I0735281

JONATHAN'S SECRET

L.A EVANS

WORKBOOK PRESS LLC
187 E Warm Springs Rd,
Suite B285, Las Vegas, NV 89119, USA

Website: https://workbookpress.com/
Hotline: 1-888-818-4856
Email: admin@workbookpress.com

Ordering Information:
Quantity sales. Special discounts are available on quantity purchases by corporations, associations, and others.
For details, contact the publisher at the address above.

Library of Congress Control Number:
ISBN-13:   978-1-954753-42-6 (Paperback Version)
                978-1-954753-43-3 (Digital Version)

REV. DATE: 24/01/2022

JONATHAN'S SECRET

A novel by

L. A. Evans

CONTENTS

Chapter One...1

Chapter Two..18

Chapter Three..39

Chapter Four...68

Chapter Five...87

Chapter Six...107

Chapter Seven...126

Chapter Eight..134

Chapter Nine...153

Chapter Ten...166

Chapter Eleven...184

CHAPTER ONE

Jonathan Broxton was a fancy man in the most prosaic use of the term. He was a tall, well-built man with big eyes, collagen puffed lips, and a square jaw. He liked to accent his eyes lightly with mascara and his lips, with pale lipstick, but it was so subtly done that—when seeing him—strangers were left to wonder, *'did he have makeup on?'* His skin was so stubble free that it looked somehow divine. He also loved the soft slinkiness of silk. His shirts and pants, supplemented by particular natural fibers to decrease wrinkles, were always silk. His socks were silk as well as his custom-made shoe tops. Everything had to match in color: either shades of black or white. His scarves and neck wear were usually the color of his mood; when it was black, no one dared talk to him before spoken to. He walked with the flare of a runway model, and his elaborate hand motions left no doubt that he was indeed a fancy man.

Thus dressed, he floated into the five star St Pierre's French restaurant he owned, located in the five star St Pierre's hotel he owned, on his way to the special table he owned. The table was at the back of the restaurant, adjacent to the kitchen wall, raised slightly, draped with black and white silk curtains and flanked by many potted white iceberg roses.

As he made his way to his table led by one

enormous bodyguard and followed by another, a young woman innocently slid her chair back from a table on her way to the powder room. The timing was such that the leg of her chair snarled Jonathan's foot, and this elegant man was propelled into the back of the lead bodyguard and subsequently onto the floor, in a most inelegant manner.

The second guard leaped at the young woman, pushed her aside and prepared to strike her as she attempted to right herself. But this was no ordinary young woman. For years, she had honed her body and mind to evenly compete with the other members of her Black Ops Team. She was tall and beautifully sculpted, and quickly recognized that she was under attack by a much larger and stronger opponent. She would not slink away as one might rightly think. Instead, she took it as a challenge and prepared for battle. She knew she would have to outthink and out-maneuver her opponent. If she attempted to match his strength, she was lost. As the bodyguard swung at her, she ducked under his arm. The force of the swing carried him slightly past her and enabled her to thrust her left hand between his legs from behind. She grabbed a handful of scrotum and squeezed hard, rendering her assailant powerless. He screeched in pain and dropped to one knee, positioning his pain ravaged face about waist high, and leaving it exposed to a roundhouse karate kick that was perfectly delivered. As her spiked heel stabbed his face, it severely ripped his lip and nose, and blood poured from his face like a broken wine decanter as he crashed to the floor.

The young woman righted herself only to find the other bodyguard speeding toward her. When he reached her, she was again able to duck beneath his fisted arm while thrusting out a leg, effectively tripping him. She accelerated his uncontrolled momentum by grasping the seat of his pants with one hand and the collar of his shirt with the other and pushing with every pound of strength she had. Lucky for her, and not so much for him, his head's progress was abruptly interrupted by the sharp edge of the bar. The resulting collision produced a dull thud, a deep gash, and a quick trip to unconsciousness. With her knees flexed and her arms raised, she examined the fruits of her labor, raised her face to the ceiling and emitted a very un-lady-like primal scream. With bent arms and hands clenched tightly into fists, she continued to scream as she performed several pirouettes.

Following a stunned silence in the room, a friend rose to his feet clapping and yelled, "Way to go, Dani!" Then, from another part of the room came an echo yell. That was followed by the ever-louder chant, "Dan-ee! Dan-ee! Dan-ee!" and suddenly, the entire room reverberated with the chant. Dani twirled and blew kisses to the crowd, exhilarated by her triumph. She soon returned to the unassuming and quiet young woman she was, examined the damage that she had wrought, and though proud, attempted to quiet the crowd by putting her index finger to her lips and waving her free arm with palm facing the crowd. The crowd chatter finally retreated to its characteristic white noise buzz and she attempted to return to her table.

Jonathan rose from his supine position on the floor where he had remained while his warriors were brought to their knees. When he saw the battle had been lost, he approached Dani. She stared defiantly at him and raised her hands again to defend herself. But his was a mission of mercy and reconciliation, and he attempted to soothe her by speaking softly, "Dani…. Dani James. I'm Jonathan Broxton. I own this place."

Dani remained in position to resume the battle and exclaimed, "And your point would be?"

"Please, Dani. I am so sorry for the behavior of these two ruffians. It was unacceptable." He received only the pose of a defiant Samurai. "Please Dani, talk to me. I am no threat to you." He held his palms vertically in a defensive position to prove his point, but also to protect himself if necessary.

In time, Dani calmed and lowered her hands but maintained her stern gaze at this fancy man she recognized, but had never met personally. "How do you know my name?" she demanded.

"Everybody knows your name now, Dani. Please, let me attempt to redeem the situation. Join me for a complimentary dinner and let me explain?"

"You sure say please a lot, mister. But I can pay for my own dinner, thank you very much!

"Yes, I know you can. But I would be honored if you joined me in my booth. It's the least I can do." Reaching out his hand, palm up, he said, "Please join me, Dani…please."

"There you go again with 'please'. Anyway, your guys need medical help."

"The doctors are attending to that as we speak. Thank you for your concern."

"I don't know, I'm still upset. These are your goons."

"Yes, I know, and you have every right to be upset. That's why, I would like you to dine with me, so that I can make amends."

"No, thanks. I'm with some friends."

"Their bill will be on the house as well." There was a positive stir from her friends' table about the offer.

Dani focused her attention upon her table of friends as she pondered, "I don't know." All she saw was heads nodding recommending an affirmative reply in anticipation of free food and drinks.

"Please join me. As you might suspect, I have an ulterior motive."

"Yeah, I thought so."

"I need your help."

"Yeah, right. You're richer than Croesus, and smarter than Da Vinci. Why would you need my help?"

"Ah! So, you know who I am?"

"Yeah, who doesn't?"

"Good. I'll explain everything as we dine. I'll provide your favorite food, your favorite drink, and your friends can eat and drink anything they want— gratis."

There were several fist pumps and "YES!" expressions from the table.

"I see you have some wise friends. In addition, you get to help a new friend with a problem. That sounds like a reasonable bargain, don't you think?"

"I have to go to the ladies' room."

"Okay, I understand." Jonathan replied with the patience of a father with a petulant child. "Then, will you join me for dinner?"

"I'll have to think about it. First, I have to pee."

Jonathan broke out in laughter and nodded his head as Dani made her way to the ladies' room to take care of business. He then made his way to his personal table.

Returning from the ladies' room, Dani

stopped at the table of friends she was sitting with before the scuffle. They all encouraged her to join Jonathan. It was such a wonderful opportunity, they thought she just couldn't possibly turn it down. Besides, they all wanted a free meal and to know what he was like in person. Maybe he would offer an award of some kind, and on and on. After some protestations, she relented and decided to join him to see what he had in mind.

Dani made her way to Jonathan's table where he welcomed her. "I have taken the liberty of ordering your favorite drink. Dinner will be delivered whenever we are ready."

She took a seat and sipped the drink. "Hmm, a Hendrick's martini straight up with three olives. That is probably what I would have ordered. Are you clairvoyant as well?"

"No, but I do my research before picking a

partner."

"Whoa, not so fast. I never said anything about being your partner in anything."

"No, of course not, and I should have said potential partner."

"Even that's going too far. What else do you know about me?"

"I know for some time you were in the CIA, and were specially trained for hand to hand combat and Black Ops. You have had training in all sorts of combat weapons and explosives. You understand and read five languages and speak three fluently. You were sent on secret special assignments frequently until your identity was compromised and you were reassigned to a desk job, which you detested and finally quit to become a detective for hire. Should I go on?"

"I'm sure you could, but that won't be necessary. I have often wondered about you. Are you really gay or is it an act?"

"Directness is another characteristic I like about you," he said as he stared directly into her eyes. "I am what I need to be. I am enormously goal oriented, and I can change to fit any occasion's need. Perhaps that is why you are confused. Most people have no doubts. You are very observant."

"Did you cause that ruckus tonight?"

"You're the one who tripped me up."

"Yeah, I know, but if it hadn't been that, it would have been something else, right?"

"Yes. I was looking for an opportunity to see you in action. To see if you were keeping in shape. The situation just fell into my lap, so to speak."

"Well, you didn't see me at my best, but your

boys were pretty inept." She paused and then, "What do you really want from me?"

"I have a project in mind for which you have characteristics that I lack, and that will enable me to pull it off."

"I'll tell you right now that I will not get involved in any illegal stuff. I can push the boundaries, but I won't step over the line."

"That's fine. I have no intention of taking advantage of little old ladies or engaging in any illegal *stuff*. It's just that there are occasions when a beautiful woman can accomplish things that are impossible for a fancy man. Especially helpful if they can take care of themselves in tight situations, which you have demonstrated tonight that you can."

"Tell me about the project."

"It involves you and me, acting as a couple,

earning the trust of various organizations that I would like to bring down. I can't tell you any more until we sign an agreement."

"How much of a couple?"

"Whatever it takes."

"I don't think I like this. See you later." She dropped her fork and began to rise.

"Dani, please sit down. You would have total say in what you do. No one will force you to do anything you don't want to. Besides, the pay will be very good."

The *'very good pay'* thing got her attention and sitting down Dani asked, "How good is very good?"

"It will be anything you ask for."

"For how long?"

"That depends on how well we do our jobs. But

I doubt it will stretch longer than a year."

Dani pondered for a moment, "Five Hundred K."

"Sold. Now let's eat. All this exertion has made me very hungry."

"What if I said a million?"

"That would be okay too."

"Then, it's a million."

"Okay."

Stunned, she sat in silence just gazing at Jonathan and the meal that was set before her. "This is exactly what I ordered last week."

"Yes, I know. You have had it four times this past year. It seems to be a favorite of yours, that's why, I ordered it for you."

"This is spooky. I don't think I like dealing with you."

"It's just research. You will learn to appreciate

my thoroughness as we proceed with the project."

"I don't know. It sounds a little too good to be true."

"I'll give you a week to think things over. Here is my room number just in case you agree to join me for further talks. Say, about eight o'clock?"

As Dani cut into her medium well-done prime rib, she said, "I'll think it over. But right now, I don't want to spoil a good meal."

"Fair enough. Let's eat."

CHAPTER TWO

Dani rang the bell to Jonathan's room and bodyguard number one opened the door. His face was badly bruised and he sported several steri-strips holding together lacerations. They leered at each other for a moment and then, she faked a punch to his midsection and he quickly stepped back to assume a defensive position. They stood, thus for a minute or so with squinted eyes, tensed bodies and tight lips, each anticipating the other's next move. And then, Dani broke into a broad smile and he soon followed. He said, "You were lucky."

She replied, "I know," and walked into the room. Both smiled.

Jonathan came rushing into the room, "Good evening, Dani. I had hoped to get here to greet you before Walter did. You never know exactly how a wounded animal will react to his erstwhile assailant.

"That's okay. We were just having a little fun together, huh, big guy?" Walter kept smiling.

"Okay. Enough of fun and games. Let's go into the study. We've got some important items to talk about."

Dani followed Jonathan into the study where another person was already sitting in a chair next to the fireplace. His pleasant face was streaked with worry lines and was topped by pure white hair, testimony to his seventy-five years. He stood as Dani entered the room and kissed her hand as Jonathan said, "Dani, I would like you to meet my father, who will be our partner in this adventure."

Dani examined this slim, six-foot gentleman, and wondered what role such a distinguished-looking old codger could play. He looked more like he needed a cane to get around than someone who could hold his own in a fight. She was not going to be a babysitter. "So, should I call you father as well?"

"That may come in time, but for the moment you may call me Henry." His steel blue eyes showed an intensity that belied his age, and his hand grip was solid.

Jonathan continued, "I rely on Henry's intellect and expertise often. Among his multiple accomplishments is an Oxford diploma. Henry knows his way around the financial markets better than anyone else I know. He is not the physical specimen he once was, his synapses are a bit withered by age, and his thinking slowed by extraneous debris, but the train always gets through even though at times it's a bit tardy. And he can still hold his own in a fight." He forgot to mention that his father's effectiveness was greatly enhanced when he swung his lead-filled ceramic cane with a ceramic dagger attached to the handle and extending into the shaft. "He has been engaged in espionage forever, and he is the one who first came up with the idea for our current project."

"Very impressive, but he won't be coming with us on dangerous assignments, will he? I mean, we don't need distractions in a tight spot."

"Now, you look here, young woman," Henry responded.

"The name is Dani, in case you've forgotten already, old man."

"Jonathan, I don't think I can work with this smart aleck child. We need someone with some brains, not just a stripper's body and a gangster's mentality."

"Now, you two kids just settle down. I've selected the two of you with great care, and I know your talents are what the project needs. You will have to work out your differences over time. Right now, we have to prepare to meet with Ramadi and convince him that we are a viable team capable of paying for the material we need."

"I don't know, Jony. They will take one look

at her, and think we're in the porn market."

"Go screw yourself, you, old fart! They will trust me more than someone who looks like they should be in a British geriatric facility."

When Henry rose from his chair and raised his cane above his head, Jonathan stepped between them and said, "Now, dammit! Stop this! I want both of you to study this material, and get it down by the time we leave in one hour. If we screw this up, we could all be dead by the end of the day. Is that understood?"

Jonathan nudged Henry back to his chair. He was holding a notebook he had been preparing for the past week, which he handed to his father. He then handed Dani the same material and scornfully glowered at her in his sternest fatherly manner.

Henry and Dani traded disapproving scowls periodically as they studied the material. At the end of an hour, Jonathan said, "Okay, time's up. Are there any questions?"

"Now, just a damn minute. I've got a couple more pages to go." Henry stammered.

"See what I mean? The old man can't cut it."

"You, silly little tart. You're lucky Jony is here or I'd knock you on your keister."

"Yeah, right. As if you could even get out of your chair, you old foggy," Dani scoffed.

"Now cut that out, both of you! I can't, for the life of me, understand why you are acting this way. The project is just too important for this silliness," Jonathan scolded. "Hurry and finish, Dad, and then we have to go."

While Henry continued to read, Dani said, "So basically, we will contact as many illegal arms dealers as we can discover, and ask if they can supply all the weapons you have listed here. Then, you will invite the ones who say they can supply everything to a reverse auction at a specified time and place. When they are all together, you intend to blow them all away in a manner unspecified at this time."

"Basically, that's the plan, yes?" Jonathan agreed.

"And the old man thought this up? Are you crazy?

"It's a good way to get rid of a lot of bad guys at the same time. We would be doing the world a great favor."

"Why don't you just pick them off one at a time and blow up their stash?"

"Clearly you see the weakness of that plan, you little ninny," Henry said while laying down the booklet. "After the first guy gets blown away, no one else would be interested. Even you should be able to see that."

"It sounds a little goofy, like its creator, but then I'm just a worker bee," Dani snorted. "By the way, I was surprised by this limerick at the end." She then proceeded to read it out loud.

"There once was a man from Pasadena,
Who found a new love at a local Cantina.
But it came as a great shock to him
When he learned his new love was Tim,
Who was suggestively dressed as Irena."

"It's kind of a funny thing to include in an RFP, don't you think?"

"Well, it adds a little levity to an otherwise

dreary document," Johnathan explained.

"And then, you're going to turn around and blow them to bits. That sounds a little strange to me."

"The limerick is mine, you little ninny," Henry spoke up.

"You're kidding, right?" Dani exclaimed, and then on second thought added, "I should have known, you, crazy old kook."

"I'd like to see what you would come up with. Probably, a dirty joke is the best you can do."

"Oh yeah? Just give me a minute. I've dabbled in verses a little bit," Dani said, while wrestling with words in her mind. After several minutes, she added, "Okay, okay. I've got one here goes:

"How about that, you, old geezer?"

"Well, I'm impressed. Maybe you are a little more than a pretty face."

Before Henry could continue, Jonathan broke in, saying, "Well, I'm glad we have reached a consensus on the plan. We can continue your poetry challenge at another time." He then called for Walter to bring the car around, and prepared to leave.

"Grab your cane, old man, so you don't fall and hurt yourself," Dani advised.

"I'll use it to smack your expensive little petard."

"Oh, so you can see without glasses," Dani

said as she wiggled her butt in front of him on her way to the limo. A moving target is hard to hit, but Henry attempted to poke her with his cane as they went.

In the car, Dani sat alone in the seat facing backwards behind the driver, facing Henry and Jonathan, who was looking pensive. "Now, let me do all the talking because I'm the one Ramadi knows, and am better prepared than the both of you. You can continue to study the material 'till we get there. It is possible he may ask you a question, but I doubt it. At any rate, don't say a word unless you are directly asked a question, okay?"

Henry and Dani both nodded their heads but said nothing. They had traveled about ten silent minutes when Walter announced, "I think someone is following us, so I'm about to start some evasive moves. Hang on."

They strapped themselves in and held tight as the limo lurched through turn after turn, with squealing tires and revving engine. The black Mercedes flew and crashed to earth following the many uneven surfaces through back alleys before returning to the main route to their destination. After several minutes, Walter announced that he could see no one following. He proceeded to their destination, and pulled to the curb in front of a brownstone. Everyone sat in the car for several silent moments. Finally, Jonathan said, "Okay. Time to get going."

They were barely out of the limo when the shooting began. At first, it was difficult to tell where the shots came from, but everyone hit the pavement or positioned himself next to the armored limo. Dani was unarmed and lay as flat as she could against the concrete. Shortly after doing so, she felt a heavy weight fall on her. Whatever it was, it covered her completely, and blotted out all light and air. It was difficult to breathe but she felt more secure being covered than relying on her perfume-scented female skin for protection.

Jonathan counseled everyone to hold their positions without firing their weapon until their attackers showed themselves. The shooting went on for several minutes, and then the squealing of tires announced the attackers' retreat. The protective blanket began to lift from Dani, and she realized that it had been Henry. "What are you doing on top of me, old man?" she yelled.

"Don't have a hissy fit. Your fancy little behind was on the ground, and I stumbled and fell down. You just happened to be underneath me and I had trouble getting up."

"You sure spend a lot of time talking about my butt."

"Don't worry about it."

"Were you trying to protect me? Is that what you were doing, or were you just trying to cop a feel?"

"Don't flatter yourself, young lady. I've seen better looking meat in cold storage."

Dani replayed the situation in her mind before saying, "Why, you, dirty old man. You were trying to protect me! I'll be damned. What a sham you are!"

"Now, listen up everyone. Get your shit together and let's see if we still have a meeting here."

Walter and Bob stayed by the limo as the

three made their way to the door and rang the bell. Ramadi soon opened the door laughing. "That was fun! You guys were not very brave but at least you are here. I thought that you would run away and our deal would be off."

"You, son of a bitch! You did that deliberately?" Jonathan protested.

"Yeah, sure. Couldn't you tell it was a hoax? We did a good job then. The bullets weren't real. When the old guy got on top of the little girl we all laughed. What a show."

Dani clenched her fist and was about to smash Ramadi in the face when Jonathan stepped between them. "You are lucky we don't take you apart, but we have a very disciplined team here. We will give you another chance of redeeming yourself. Your explanation better be good, cause my guys have real bullets in real guns, and they are prepared to use them."

"Ha, ha, Jonathan. It was just a joke and a way to make sure you are the type of team we want to deal with. I had to see if you ran away at the first sign of combat."

"You are just lucky. My guys showed restraint and didn't shoot back. That would have made you look pretty stupid, wouldn't it?"

"Whatever you say, Jony. It *could* have turned out badly, but you seem a disciplined team, so we might as well continue with our discussions. I hope we are in agreement on that. Please accept my apologies. Follow me into the parlor, so we can have some wine, bread and cheese, and start over. Okay?"

Jonathan checked with his partners who nodded yes, and they all proceeded into the house to determine if Ramadi was someone who could be made to believe that they could afford the weapons and explosives they needed to fulfill their project.

When the group was settled with appetizers and wine Jonathan handed Ramadi a booklet several pages thick and said, "I have prepared a detailed list of the items that we need and the conditions that go with it. We will be giving a similar package to several other potential suppliers, and in two months we will conduct a meeting where all attendees will submit bids for the materials. We intend to award the contracts to the lowest bidder. In the meantime, during the last two weeks before the auction, we will personally visit each bidder to examine the materials to assess the quality and completeness of the bidder's materials. Anyone not measuring up at that time and without a compelling excuse will be eliminated from consideration. We are prepared to guarantee our ability to pay the required amount to the satisfaction of each bidder prior to their acquisition of the materials. This is all included in the booklet that you have just received. Is all of this clear, Ramadi?"

"There is quite a lot to digest here, Mr. Broxton. I must have my people examine it carefully before we make a commitment," Ramadi said as he hefted the booklet. "I'm not sure that I would be willing to meet together with a group of people willing to supply C-4, semtex, grenade launchers, and remote-detonation pipe bombs."

"Why not? You all know each other anyway, or nothing would ever get done," Jonathan countered.

"I don't think I like it."

"Accommodations could be made I suppose if your feelings are duplicated."

Ramadi frowned and surveyed the Broxton team. "You are a very pretty woman my dear. What do you do for the team, provide entertainment?"

Dani gritted her teeth and replied, "I do what is necessary."

"That's nice. Have you ever killed anyone?"

"I would shoot you without a second's hesitation if the situation required it," she answered with a flat affect and expressionless face.

Momentarily surprised, Ramadi decided no further questions needed to be asked, and team Broxton prepared to leave.

Jonathan shook Ramadi's hand and while maintaining eye contact said, "By the way, if we ever come here again and hear gunshots we will respond with every weapon we have directly into this house and continue shooting until our ammunition is all gone and no window or door remains intact. We look forward to your reply to our RFP. Have a nice day."

CHAPTER THREE

Jonathan and Company found themselves in a rather seedy part of town as they attempted to locate another of their potential weapons suppliers. All they were given was a street name and a number. "This looks like a strange place for a big time dealer, but the numbers are right," he mused.

The first indication that the place was a bit odd was Sam's Butcher Shop whose motto was flashing in neon: *'You can't beat our meat!'* Across the street was Phil's Butcher Shop exclaiming, *'In case of fire grab your meat and beat it.'* All of which brought a smile to everyone's lips and incredulity to their minds.

But things were to get even bolder at Virgin Mary's strip club whose motto was *'Come fall into our crack.'* In the next block was Connie's Chicken where potential customers were asked to *'Come eat our cocks.'* And across the street was Dick's Slobber Pole'. The owner apparently felt no motto was necessary. That was too much for the gang, and they decided to concentrate on the numbers and forget about the unusual play on words.

When they finally reached the number they were looking for, they found Mike's Nut House with its motto, *'Mike has delicious nuts.'* They almost turned and left but they had come this far and felt they needed to see things through.

Walt found a place to park a few doors down from Mike's, and the three partners got out. "You better stay with the car, Walt. This is a strange neighborhood, and we won't be far away."

"Yes, sir. We'll keep an eye out."

Just before reaching Mike's Nut House, the partners were confronted by a bearded fellow with earrings, and tattoos scattered about his face and bare arms. In his right hand was a Glock 9mm pointed at Jonathan's stomach. As he opened his mouth, they were nearly blinded by the sun reflected from the diamonds embedded in his front teeth. "Stop right here, and give me all your valuables, including that briefcase. Make it snappy or I'll blow your heads off. I ain't kidding. Move it!"

"Whoa! Take it easy, buddy. We're just here to see Mike. Do you know him?" Jonathan was able to push through a very tight throat.

"Shut up, and throw all your stuff in this bag, fairy-man, or I'll shoot all these turds. You choose. I don't give a fuck!"

Henry had raised his lead filled cane as he raised his hands in response to their assailant's request. As Jonathan made a move to hand over the briefcase and the thief reached to receive it, Henry brought the cane down with a ferocity matching his anger, striking the assailant's wrist with a dreadful thud which was only partially camouflaged by his scream of pain. The bad guy dropped his weapon, and Henry swung his cane again this time striking the side of the assailant's knee pulverizing his kneecap and sending the guy to the ground screaming profanities.

Walt and Bob arrived just in time to collect the defeated warrior and drag him away. Jonathan said, "Give him a good talking to, punch him around a bit, and then let him go."

"Okay, boss. We'll take good care of him," Walt promised with a sardonic smile.

Henry had acted before Dani and Jonathan, and the battle was resolved so quickly that the incident barely made a ripple in their progress to Mike's Nut House.

As they walked, Dani said to Henry, "Wow that was great. I guess you won't be such a drag on us after all, old man."

"Well, thank you, my dear. You are very sweet."

"Don't get too excited, I'm not about to jump your bones," Dani sneered.

Henry seared her with his sky blue eyes, and with a barely detectable grin said, "Pity."

Dani displayed a grin through a flushed face. She was barely unable to stifle the image of the two of them together romantically. How outrageous, she thought!

As they opened the door of the shop, a young man stood behind the counter that conjured the image of that *'What, me worry?'* guy. You know, the full, round, freckled face with a big smile exposing a noticeable gap between the front two teeth. It was Jonathan's sincere hope that this Alfred E. Newman look-alike was not Mike.

"Hey, buddy. Can you tell me where Mike is?" Jonathan asked the young man. He was standing in front of a sign reading *'Mike's nuts are tasty.'*

"I don't know," said the young man without looking up.

"Do you expect him back today?"

"Who?" the young man mumbled.

Jonathan began to believe that the boy was in fact the Mad Magazine character, and changed the topic he might more fully grasp. "What is your name, young man?"

Finally, looking up at Jonathan, the boy said, "Alfred. Who wants to know?"

Jonathan was struck dumb for a moment by the coincidence. With a broad smile he said, "I'm Jonathan Broxton. I am supposed to meet with Mike about a business matter."

"Don't know nothin' about that," Alfred replied.

Knowing by now he would have to sneak up on Alfred to get a straight answer, Jonathan asked, "What kind of nut is your favorite?"

"Oh, I like the round soft ones that are kind of fuzzy." Jonathan was puzzled and inquired, "What kind of nut is that?"

"Mike's," the boy replied.

Jonathan's potty brain probably colored his understanding of Alfred's statement as he exclaimed in amazement, "You like to eat Mike's nuts?"

"I don't know. Nuts is nuts, ain't they?" the boy said with a smile.

"Yes… Yes of course." Jonathan stammered

attempting to clean up his imagery. He was looking to his partners for help, but receiving only smiles, savoring the predicament Jonathan found himself in. This very bright man was seemingly being defeated in a word game by this simple boy.

"You seem to have a one track mind, and we're sliding down a slippery slope here," Jonathan said with an aggravated wave of his hand.

"Yeah, the slippery slope. That's the fun of it ain't it."

"What is it with all this sexual innuendo?" Jonathan stammered.

"Hey, fairy man, I don't do that."

"Do what?" Jonathan frowned.

"Why are you asking me all these dirty questions anyway?"

Turning to his cohorts Jonathan asked in desperation, "What is he talking about?"

Walt was frantically pointing to his rear end while mouthing the words, in your endo. Jonathan finally realized that innuendo was probably a new word for Alfred, and in desperation said, "Okay… Alfred, let's start again. Do you know where Mike lives?"

"Yeah, sure," Alfred said with a shrug, arms out to his sides with palms up an open mouth, and a flabbergasted look on his face, obviously thinking, "What a stupid question."

Jonathan looked stoically at the young man, and after several seconds decided to move the subject a little slower, "Could you give us his address?"

The young man stood with a quizzical look on his face as he attempted to put an answer to the question. Jonathan decided to simplify the question, "Do you know where he lives?"

"He lives with me," the boy said triumphantly.

"But you don't remember the address?"

"Yes."

"I wonder if you would be willing to take us there," Jonathan begged, still receiving no help from the amused bystanders.

"No."

"Why not?"

"I don't have no car."

"How about if I drive my car?"

"You can drive your car if you want."

"No, I mean if I drive my car with you in it, will you show me where you live?" Jonathan said slowly and with impeccable annunciation.

"You'll have to let me close up first."

"That's fine. I'll wait for you to close up so that I can take you home."

"Why didn't you say so instead of asking all those dirty questions?"

"Yes, of course. That was pretty dumb of me, wasn't it?" Jonathan conceded.

The young man shook his head at the numb-skull that was about to take him home and began the close up routine.

"Which way do we go?" Walt inquired after all parties were in the limo.

The boy pointed and Walt took off in that direction. After traveling several blocks, Walt inquired, "How much further?"

"Well, it would have been shorter if you had taken a left back there," Alfred exclaimed pointing with his thumb.

Walt slammed on the brakes and the limo screeched to a stop, "Get up here in the front seat next to me. Right...now!"

"Okay, okay. You don't have to get mad at me just because you missed the turn. Jeez."

"Okay. Now, here are the rules from now on, and if you break the rules, I'm going to break your head. Do you understand, freckles?" Walt demanded.

"My name's Alfred," Alfred reminded the impatient Walt.

"I know what your fucking name is, kid. Just sit there and do as I tell you."

"Walt, take it easy. He's not the brightest bulb in the marquee you know," Jonathan implored.

"Yeah, like you did so well communicating with him... sir," Walt sneered, glaring in the mirror.

"What rules?" Alfred asked with a worried look on his face.

"I'm going to start driving and at the end of each block you are going to tell me whether or not to turn, and if so in which direction, got it?"

"I guess so. Turn left at the next corner.

Don't hit me, okay?"

"Damn right I'll hit you if you don't follow the rules!" Walt snarled.

"That doesn't sound like a fun game," the boy frowned.

Walt glared at him and said, "Don't fuck with me, kid."

After negotiating several turns and angry looks, Alfred said, "This is where I live."

Walt pulled over to a stop and said, "What floor and room does Mike live?"

"I don't know," Alfred confessed with a sheepish look on his face while ducking his head under his arm for protection from an expected hit.

"You said this is where you and he live. Is

that right or not, goddamn it?"

"He lives here, but I don't know the number. Jeez, you made me pee my pants. You're so mean!" Alfred screamed.

Walt leapt from the limo, hustled around to the passenger's side and angrily grabbed Alfred by the arm and dragged him, wet trousers and all, toward the building. His astonished entourage tagged close behind. "I'm tired of you, boy. You're going to take me directly to Mike's door and bang on it. If he doesn't come and answer the door, I'm going to beat you to death right there and feed your dead body to the dogs. Now, get your dumb ass moving!"

"Walt, please take it easy," Dani pleaded. "He's doing the best he can."

Tears were streaming down Alfred's

chunky cheeks as the group reached the penthouse, and Alfred banged on the door as if his life depended on it. The boy cowered against the door frame and kept saying softly, "Be here Mike.... be here Mike or I'm dog meat."

Finally, the boy's prayers were answered and Mike opened the door and said, "What the fuck is all the noise about?"

"I'm Jonathan Broxton. We have an appointment."

The boy slithered around behind Mike saying, "This mother fucker said he was going to kill me and feed me to the dogs... and that one talked dirty to me," Alfred informed his savior.

"It's okay, Alfred. I'll take care of these guys. You go with Mansfred, take a shower, and then grab a bite to eat, okay?"

When Alfred felt safe at the other end of the room, he turned, stuck his thumbs in his ears, stuck out his tongue and wiggled his fingers as an act of defiance toward his antagonists. The Broxton group could only smile and silently cheer for the freckle faced kid who was paddling as fast as he could while missing at least one of his oars.

"Please come in, all of you," Mike said with a hand motion toward his living room. "I hope Alfred didn't cause you too much trouble."

"No, not at all. We could tell he was struggling a bit."

"He's just a little below normal I guess, but he functions quite well at the store. I give him as much responsibility as he can handle. I'm all he has since our mom and dad passed," Mike explained.

"You seem to have done quite well with him, Mike," Jonathan replied as he surveyed the apartment. He was impressed with the acid stained concrete floor, oriental rugs, and the exposed galvanized ventilation system. The Italian leather couch, ottoman and chairs were strategically placed to call attention to the enormous lion-ornamented stone fireplace that rose fifteen feet to the ceiling. His gaze swept through the room which was very ornately decorated, passed the grand piano and floor to ceiling windows with views of the river and city lights just a block away. The dining room was furnished with a Chippendale antique dining table, chairs and hutch. And of course, there was the chef-quality kitchen… Wolf, Sub Zero, Miele, Asko, etc., and stainless steel, quartz and cherry wood everywhere. A hallway led to the bedroom and bathroom suite where Alfred had retreated to regroup.

"Your accommodations are very impressive, Mike," Jonathan praised. "Something like I might have chosen."

"Thank you, Jonathan. Knowing your reputation, I'm particularly pleased."

Jonathan said, "Allow me to introduce Dani and Henry, my trusted associates."

"I am happy to meet you both. Please have a seat."

"We were a bit mystified by the neighborhood, and I must say a bit worried about what you would be like." Jonathan said. "I'm glad to say that those misgivings have now been alleviated."

"Thank you. When dad and mom first

opened the Nut House twenty- five years ago, the neighborhood was much more urbane. But the years were not kind to the area, and some rather seedy folks moved in. In desperation, the old timers either moved out or began to create businesses and names that would be more in keeping with the new inhabitants, and thus keep the area from slipping even further to the dark side."

"Judging from your accommodations, you seem to be doing just fine, Mike."

"This is only possible because of interactions with fellows such as yourself Jonathan.

As Mansfred delivered the refreshments, Jonathan replied, "Which brings me to the purpose of our meeting. We need the weapons and ammunitions that are specified in this booklet for a project we are planning. Study it carefully and get back to me as soon as possible, so that an auction involving other interested parties can be arranged to choose the final supplier."

Mike thumbed through the document while the visitors quenched their thirst and appetite. Looking up, he said, "This is pretty detailed and the variety is quite extensive. I don't think the list of potential suppliers will be large."

"Perhaps not but competition often turns up more than one might rightfully expect."

After a few drinks, food, and conversation, Mike looked at Dani and said, "And what is it that you bring to the table Dani?"

"I'm the muscle."

Mike began to laugh and said, "You're kidding, right?"

"No. That's my role."

"Then who are the goons at the door?"

"They are here for backup."

"Wow! That's pretty amazing. Show me." Mike continued as he knelt beside the coffee table, put his elbow down with his hand raised.

"Are you challenging me to an arm wrestle? Dani questioned.

"That's right. Show me what you got."

"You better watch what you ask for," Henry interrupted. "You may get much more than you can handle."

"And what are you, the resident philosopher old man?"

"You're on, shit face," Dani said angrily,

protecting Henry. She then moved into position, grabbed Mike's hand in hers and assumed a firm grip.

"Anytime you're ready, little lady," Mike smirked, as Alfred raced into the room shouting, "Give it to her, Mikie. Show her who's the boss."

"Geez, Alfred, you're in your underwear. Go back and get dressed for god's sake."

Dani slowly increased the intensity of her grip and applied pressure to Mike's hand and arm. Mike held his own to see how much power Dani had, allowing her to push his hand well past the center point.

Sensing that Mike needed some help Alfred screamed again, "Give it to her Mikie. She's a pussy."

When Mike thought he had Dani's

measure, he began his own power push while looking directly into her eyes, expecting to see the confidence drain, to be replaced by fear and pain. Seconds after returning to the center point, he felt Dani's reserve power kick in, and the momentum slowly returned to her. He then began to exert all the power he had in order to finish her off quickly. But pushing with everything he had could not reverse Dani's momentum. After several minutes of anguished struggle, she forced his hand to the table with a thud.

"Nice try, Mike, but as I said I'm the muscle."

"Well, I'll be damned," Mike said rubbing his arm. "Two out of three?"

"No, thanks. That wouldn't be lady-like."

"Geez, Mikie you let the evil one beat you," Alfred moaned and sat silently with a very forlorn look on his face. He appeared to be the defeated one.

Dani felt so sorry for him that she moved slowly over to Alfred and lovingly stroked his face with her hand as she said, "You know, Alfred, you're so sweet I could just eat you up."

At which point Alfred jumped to his feet, and with extreme fear in his eyes screamed, "I told you, Mikie. They want to cut me into pieces and eat me like a dog."

"I know, Alfred. You better get your ass into the other room before they attack. I'll take care of these animals."

Alfred slammed the door behind him and was activating the last of three locks by the time

Mike had finished his warning. "Ha, ha, ha," Alfred yelled from behind the barricade, "You animals can't eat me now. You take care of 'em Mikie, and then we'll have *them* for supper."

"Okay, Alfred. I'm taking care of them. You just relax, okay?" Mike yelled to Alfred. He then turned to his guests, "You know, Alfred is a good kid and means no harm. It's just that his head is filled with words and ideas that randomly travel their individual journeys, and sometimes they pour out in ways that we mere mortals have trouble deciphering. I hope you're not offended by that last outburst."

"Of course not," Dani replied, "he truly is a delightful child. I could have chosen my words a little more carefully."

After the battle of the sexes, the group ate and drank for a few silent moments. Mike then rose and placed his hand on Jonathan's shoulder. He began massaging in a manner which implied a closer relationship than the situation appropriately warranted. Looking directly into Jonathan's eyes he said, "Why don't you dismiss your compatriots, so you and I can get to know each other better?"

Jonathan tensed as he gently slid Mike's hand aside and said, "This is probably a good time for all of us to leave."

"I hope my gesture didn't offend you, Jonathan," Mike said apologetically.

"No, not at all," Jonathan replied. "It's just that business is business and pleasure is pleasure, and I don't mix the two." After a brief pause, he continued, "Okay, troops let's be on our way. Thank you Mike for your hospitality. Please review the document and get back to me within the week."

Before closing the door behind him, Jonathan turned to Mike and said, "We'll have a blast after the auction." He had in mind a different kind of blast than Mike envisioned.

CHAPTER FOUR

The three partners sat silently in the limo before Henry said, "Well, that was interesting. Different than the previous one but exciting in its own way. You know, Jony, it would have been alright if you had stayed."

"Yeah, I know but the way it ended just didn't sit well. I like the guy, I guess, but I keep thinking about the end of the auction, and if my premise is correct, then they are all bad guys who the world would be better off without. Why start something now, and then blow it to hell?"

"You have a point. Still, a bird in the hand…"

"I thought you didn't necessarily like boys." Dani chimed in.

"That's correct. The external genitalia shouldn't determine one's affection for another, should it?"

"That's disgusting. I don't even want to think about it. Can we change the subject? Oh, I know. I have a limerick for you, old man. Think you can match it?"

"Sure. Show me what 'ya got."

"Here goes:

There once was a man from Nantucket,
Who told his boss to go stuff it.
But he feared for his life,
When he told his sweet wife,
Cause she pummeled his head with a bucket.

There. Let's see you beat that."

"Not too bad for a beginner, but I think I have one that'll top that:

There once was man named Bonaparte,
Who deservedly died of a broken heart.
World domination was his goal, And
countless people paid a heavy toll.
But justice prevailed, and all his evil plans fell apart.

Now this one has some social relevance to it!"

"Yeah, you're right, but that's not what I was aiming for."

"Anyway, changing the subject a little," Henry interjected. "Thank you for coming to my rescue back there. Although, I'm perfectly capable of taking care of myself."

"Yeah, I know, but he really disrespected me as well as you, and you stood up for me too."

"I just didn't want you to hurt the guy until we got his weapons."

"Yeah, right."

"Really. Jonathan told me the way you banged up the guys at the restaurant."

Dani responded, "I was just lucky and they were overconfident."

"You are such an attractive little package that you must surprise most people with your strength."

"Well thanks, you, old darling. You are stronger and more agile than your age would suggest. Maybe that's why we make a better team than I first thought."

"That brings up a good point, Dani. Why

don't you move in with me and dad?"

"What? That's crazy!" Dani protested.

"Not really," Jonathan replied. "We will be seeing a lot of each other for the next few months and it would save a lot of time and logistics if we're all together."

"That's still crazy."

"There are other reasons. For example, it would save you money, and you would be safer."

"Why is security an issue?"

"As more and more bad guys get to know us as a team, your isolation will make you more vulnerable and that worries me."

"Hmm... I never thought of that. I've been looking for a new place, and it seems they want to convert the apartments to condos. How would it work?"

"I have had one suite closed off for some time. It's completely separate from my and dad's suites, but can be opened to the main rooms just as ours do. You would have complete privacy when you want it and yet we can be together for planning and other things on a moment's notice. The three of us would be protected by the best security system that money can buy. What do you think?"

"I'd like to see the suite."

After they arrived at Jonathan's penthouse, they began the tour. "Anticipating your move, I have had a crew working for the past two weeks tweaking the place: new paint, carpet, complete new bath and closets. I had the kitchenette totally redone and the great room has new furniture and the latest in electronics, television, computer and home theatre. You would be self-sufficient if you never came out of your suite."

"This is beautiful. About twice the size of my current place. But I don't think I could afford it."

"It wouldn't cost you anything. You would be doing me a favor if you agree to move in."

"Are you serious? she gasped.

"Of course, I'm serious."

After a minute of reflection, she said, "I'll move in tomorrow."

"Then, it's a deal. Now, as to the security. The floor below us contains our security and information teams. That's where Bob and Walter live. The place is filled with the latest counter measures and protection schemes along with Cloud computing which gives us the internet world at our fingertips. That's how I knew about your eating habits, and the fact that you were looking for a new apartment. It is absolutely impossible for someone to get onto or past that floor without being detected and destroyed."

"How about the roof and the windows?" Dani mocked.

"The windows are bullet and grenade proof. The roof has a helipad that is protected by satellite and appropriate weaponry for every conceivable attack, except an atom bomb. Trust me, we are safe here."

"That's both scary and comforting."

"I haven't said anything about our research arm. It's there, too. But enough of the tour. Let's go back to the great room and discuss the day, and what the next few days will consist of."

On their way to the great room, Jonathan said,

"Oh, I forgot the work out room. It's right through here. I'm afraid there is just one room for the three of us right now. If that doesn't work out, we can make some changes. As you can see, there is at least one of everything dad and I use. If there is something missing, just let me know. We can schedule separate times or mix and match. I'm open to any suggestions."

"Holy smokes! This is great. I feel like a kid at Christmas time. Just quickly looking around, I can't think of anything that isn't here." The Gold Gym apparatus was almost as big as Dani's bedroom. There was a top of the line free weight bench and weights, adjustable resistance bike, a small hardwood floor for aerobic dance moves and a stereo system that could blow your ears off. There was much more but that would only be of interest to those gym rats who are only happy when they are panting hard and sweating four to six hours a day.

Dani was overwhelmed and gave Jonathan a hug and a kiss on the cheek, and added, "This is wonderful! Thank you so much."

Then, Henry piped in, "Don't I get a kiss too?"

Jonathan continued into the great room as Dani wheeled around and said playfully, "I have one for you too, you little pumpkin." She then gave him a friendly kiss on the lips, then started to turn and follow Jonathan.

Henry reached out and held her by the shoulders, then slid his hand around her waist and pulled her close and kissed her on the lips very long and affectionately. This was not out of character for him because from their first meeting he was completely taken by her charm, beauty, athleticism and intellect. From the very beginning he felt she was just a perfect female and was greatly disappointed when she attacked him verbally and he was forced to defend himself in kind.

Dani on the other hand was completely surprised by Henry's affectionate kiss and was shocked even more by her reaction to it. As his kiss lingered on her lips, she began to feel a familiar but unexpected vibration just below her mid-section. *How can this be?* she thought, as she pulled away briefly and gazed up at him with a quizzical look on her face. This was the same old man she had been belittling from the day she met him. She thought to herself, *'What's going on here, he's old enough to be my dad, and I'm becoming aroused by his kisses, this* is *crazy.'*

Nevertheless, she found herself uncontrollably wrapping her hands around his waist, pulling him close to her and changing her friendly kiss to one more in keeping with a passionate lover.

Henry was so startled that he went weak in the

knees and he felt his own midsection vibrating in a way that he hadn't experienced for several years. He was pleased but embarrassed by his obvious arousal and attempted to pull away. Dani held tightly not allowing him to move as she drew pleasure from the bulge in Henry's trousers.

Dani asked slyly, "Henry… is that a banana in your pocket?"

His face flushed but he stood tall and proudly exclaimed, "Uh… I can assure you, my dear, that the bulge in my trousers is not caused by a piece of fruit.

Dani laughed and then released her grip on him and moved away as she examined him from head to toe. She could not contain her amused admiration of this conflicted older man who stood before her clearly displaying his condition; proud of his accomplishment, but at the same time embarrassed by its public display. She smiled broadly and said, "Oh, really. No, banana, huh? I didn't think that was possible for a man of your age."

"Well, it's not common but under special circumstances anything is possible."

"So, you're saying that our kissing was a special circumstance for you?"

"By definition, I guess."

Under examination, Henry squirmed and tried to camouflage his condition as best he could, "Don't make fun of me now, you, little black widow."

She gazed at him quizzically, "I'm not making fun, I'm just surprised by what has just happened to both of us. But I guess, joy can make people do things they might not otherwise do."

"Yes, that probably explains it, and while my condition and your mental state were under examination and amazement, I'm sorry to say, the banana has just fallen from the tree," Henry replied.

Dani smiled briefly, "I'm kind of glad for that, Henry. Who knows what might have happened."

"Well, I do hope we can try to cultivate a new crop sometime. In the meantime, we better join Jonathan in the other room."

As they entered the great room, Jonathan said, "What the hell were you doing out there?"

"We were discussing farming... actually growing bananas," Henry replied with a smile as he glanced briefly at Dani.

"Where in the hell did that come from?" Jonathan wanted to know. "We are just as surprised as you are, Jonathan," Dani laughed.

"You took so much time that I'm on my second

brandy, and now I don't really feel like discussing business any more. I need relaxation."

Henry added with a smile, "I could use a little of relaxation myself right now."

"Do you play chess, Dani?" Jonathan asked.

"I know how the pieces are supposed to move but I don't know much about the strategy of the game."

"Too bad. I was thinking I would like to engage you in a game of cerebral chess."

"What do you mean?"

"With cerebral chess, you don't play in the physical world, it's strictly played in the mind."

"That sounds kind of weird. Why would anyone want to do that?"

"Well, it's a challenge. Hard to do, and not many people can do it."

"How does it go?"

"Say, I'm white and I open by saying, I move the queen's pawn to queen four. Then, you would call out your move with black. Say, maybe the same move as mine, or something that you thought might be better defense against that opening. From then on, each of us would have to remember the current position of every piece on the board in order to make the next logical move. As the moves accumulate, the difficulty mounts exponentially, but you proceed until someone gives up or gets checkmated just as in physical chess."

"That seems impossible. No one could proceed more than three or four moves," Dani exclaimed. "Then, there would be a disagreement on the current position of pieces and neither person could prove their contention."

"Yes, we found that to be a problem early on. There needs to be a referee to move pieces on a board or computer to keep everyone honest. Dad taught me the game years ago and beat the hell out of me for years. But now, the tables have turned slightly."

"I can still hold my own, but perhaps you have a slight edge now," Henry admitted.

"That's well beyond me," Dani confessed. "I'd like to see the two of you play sometime, but not tonight. I'm getting a bit weary and I've got to drive home."

"No you don't. This is where you live now, remember?" Henry reminded her.

"But I don't have any clothes, toothbrush, makeup, etc."

"You forget the power on the floor below. They determined and purchased everything you will need to stay. There may be some duplication with things you have at home, but everything you need is in your suite. Go take a look. If something you need isn't there we will have it delivered within thirty minutes. Guaranteed."

"You guys are completely amazing. I think I have died and gone to heaven. I'm so happy right now that I'm doing crazy things. I feel like I have found a new family."

She then gave Jonathan a kiss on the cheek as before, and then turned to Henry to do the same, however Henry turned his head slightly so that their lips once again met. Henry's kiss lasted longer than Jonathan's by mutual consent.

As Dani moved toward her suite, Henry called after her, "Welcome home sweetheart." Tears of happiness welled in her eyes as she turned back to them. She was so overcome by emotion that she could not speak. She just smiled with tears running down her cheeks and waved her hand as she disappeared into her new home.

CHAPTER FIVE

Dani scurried about her old apartment tying tags on all the items to be moved including dishes. Two young men arrived and she opened the door for them.

"Please, come in guys. Everything is tagged. Blue for storage, green for the new apartment, and red just leave where it is. Here is the name and address for the storage units and the new apartment. You'll have to place the stuff in the storage unit anyway you see fit. They have instructions to give you the key. At the hotel, you will just off load the stuff on the dock. The guys there will take it up to my room. So, where do you want to start?"

The tall, good-looking guy with broad shoulders, bright eyes and a winning smile stepped forward and examined the information. "Hi, I'm Roger. I'm in charge of the move. If you have any questions, just ask." As he turned to begin the heavy lifting, he said, "Thanks for organizing things so well. It will make the move go a lot faster. We'll start with the storage stuff, and then the apartment stuff, so it won't slow you down. I imagine you're anxious to get moved in."

"You've got that right, Roger," Dani responded and stepped out of the way. "I don't have any questions right now, and you look like you could move a mountain all by yourself. So, have at it!

"Yes, ma'am. I'm built for the job. By the way,

St. Pierre is a hotel, isn't it?"

"Yes, it is. But I'm renting a small apartment there at least for a while."

"I didn't know they did that. You must have an *in* of some kind."

"Yeah, I've been working for the owner for a while."

"Jonathan Broxton?"

"Yeah. Do you know him?"

"No, not personally, but everyone knows who he is. You're a lucky girl or very good at what you do. I hear he's pretty hard-nosed. Good luck to you."

"Thanks, Roger. It's been great so far."

"I understand he's into something, rather

unusual for him."

"Where did you hear that?"

"Oh, it's just general scuttlebutt, I guess."

"That's interesting."

"Yes, and so are you, pretty lady."

Dani shooed him away with her hand but she watched his graceful movement as he walked away. There was something about him that piqued her interest. Occasionally, when you meet a person for the first time, they seem to be someone you would like to get to know better, and they reflect that feeling as well. Roger was such a person for Dani. She thought about him as she walked into the bathroom and began cleaning. As she began to clean the shower, she idly pictured Roger and herself in the shower together, lathering each other. Such daydreams often make nasty jobs appear to move more quickly. She smiled and hummed as she went about her cleaning.

As time wore on, she answered questions as they came up, but they were few, and she was able to clean both the bath and the kitchen by the time Roger came to her and said, "We have everything loaded except the bed that wasn't labeled. What should we do with that?"

Dani scarcely looked him in the eye because she only saw him in his naked state in the shower, and it made her blush. They walked together from room to room checking things out, and she then said, "Yes, it looks like you got everything out, alright."

"Yes, ma'am. But what about the bed?"

"Yes, the bed." Dani then hesitated because her mind suddenly became involuntarily preoccupied by a different adventure with her new best friend. An internal debate raged whether or not to follow through with an idea that had preoccupied her since she first laid eyes on him. Was it the pheromones or was it just his natural good looks and potential for making beautiful babies that attracted her? She couldn't decide. After an awkward pause, she said, "Would you tell your helper that I have a special job for you and you'll be out shortly?"

Roger couldn't imagine what she had in mind, the whole apartment was empty except for the bed and he wasn't about to help with the clean-up. But he did what she asked, and then said, "What do you want me to do?"

She then walked over to the door and locked it. Turning around slowly, she said, "I have a question for you. Would you have any use for the bed and all the bedding?"

Roger thought that was a strange question, but after checking things out said, "Yeah, as a matter of fact, I could use a new bed. I've been sleeping on a blow up mattress for the last six months. That would be great."

"You look like you're in good shape, nothing seemed to be too heavy for you. Are you tired?"

"Four years of college football, the last two as a starting linebacker will do that for a guy. No, I'm not tired at all. What do you have in mind?"

"Would you mind taking off your shirt?"

"The boss wants us to always stay in uniform while we're working."

"Well, technically, you're not working right now, are you?"

"No, I guess not. But why do you want me to

take my shirt off?"

"I just wanted to see you with your shirt off." She lowered and tilted her head and coyly looked up at him with an ever so innocent look. "Is that okay?"

"Yeah, I guess so." He was a little confused but his mind began to race as he recalled more experienced movers talk about some of their fantasies about the beautiful women they had moved. Dani was definitely a very beautiful woman. He began to hope that today was his lucky day. He examined Dani closely and felt like he was about to explode.

He knew she would like what she saw, and he didn't mind making such a beautiful young woman happy. So, he slowly unbuttoned his shirt and threw it on the bed and playfully struck a body builder's pose with arms arched at his sides with fists and teeth clenched tightly.

"Aha! I thought so. You are beautifully built and very sexy."

"Thank you, ma'am. I'm kind of proud of the way I look."

"And well, you should be," Dani said as she moved to him and began to release his belt and unbutton his pants.

"Whoa, ma'am. What are you doing?" He asked as he instinctively reached down and grabbed her hand.

"Well, I'm giving you my bed and all the bedding. Don't you think you owe me something for it?"

"Yes, ma'am. How much do you want for it?"

"I want you to make love to me on the bed before you take it. It will give me a lovely memory of the apartment and the beautiful young man that helped me move."

"Well yeah, sure. That would be great."

"Great. Now let's get those pants off."

As the pants hit the floor, Roger stood straight, and while he was embarrassed, there was an air of pride and confidence in the way he held his head high and let all of his equipment magnificently display itself.

Dani surveyed this young Adonis, and newly installed draperies in her new apartment crossed her mind. Specifically, how the designer had said they were very well hung. Now, she knew a different meaning for the word. She reached out for his hand and led him to the bed. "Now, you just lie here as I prepare myself."

With eyes wide with excitement and his heart furiously beating, he lay on the bed and said, "Yes, ma'am. You are absolutely awesome. I think I must be dreaming."

Dani seductively undressed and then moved slowly to the bed, knelt next to him and playfully ran her hand over his body from head to toe. She then straddled him and they began a series of activities designed to provide each other memories for a lifetime.

When total satisfaction was achieved, the two naked bodies lay entwined with each other, and the sweaty contact was mutually enjoyed for several minutes. Neither one of them wanted to let go of the other. The feeling was too precious to think about stopping. What had started out as a whim, turned out to be a very memorable treasure, more reminiscent of a wedding night.

Dani was first to speak as she raised her head from his chest. "Thank you, Roger. It feels wonderful to be here with you. It will be difficult to tear myself away. I haven't felt this good in a long time. You are very special."

"Thank you, Dani. You are the most beautiful woman I can imagine. I swear this day has become the day I will always remember. I wish it would go on forever."

"As wonderful as that feeling is right now, I don't think it's in the cards. Our lives are just too different." She then gave him a long, gentle kiss, and several loving pecks on the lips, things that one might only expect from a couple who have been romantically linked for some time. They both slowly put their clothes back on while constantly watching each other to prolong this special event in their memories.

Roger called his helper and they hauled the bed to the truck. When he returned, Dani said, "You know, if there is anything else in the truck, not ticketed for the apartment, which you could use, I would like you to have it."

"Oh, I couldn't do that, Dani. You are just too generous. I would take everything just to keep this day alive."

"I'm very serious, Roger. I just knowing you have it would make me very happy."

They said goodbye at the doorway, and shared their last tender kiss with tears in their eyes.

Later that evening, after the move was completed, and Dani had put everything in place in the new apartment, she joined Jonathan in the main living room. She was humming and virtually skipping about the room exhibiting a level of excitement that Jonathan had rarely seen. "Well, my dear Dani. You seem to be in great spirits this evening. Are you happy that all the moving is done?"

"Yes, partly, but it's a lot more than that."

"Please share."

"Oh, I don't know. It's something that is completely out of character for me. I really shouldn't talk about it. I'm not sure I'm very proud of it."

"Okay. You be the judge, but you seem to be ready to burst if you don't talk about it."

"You seem determined to drag it out of me, damn you."

"Yeah, right."

"I seduced a young man on my old bed at the

apartment today," she blurted out.

"Whoa! You little slut. Tell me more. How did that happen?"

"I won't go into the details cause that's just too private."

"Whatever you're comfortable with. But I think it would be good for you to talk about it. Helps put things into proper perspective."

"He was the lead mover, and was tall, dark and handsome. I just couldn't take my eyes off him all day. After the packing was complete, I didn't want it to end the usual way, so I undressed him and made love to him. It turned out to be very special."

"I'm sure that is something he will treasure… love in the afternoon with an older woman. You are such a cougar. I didn't think you were that impulsive, but it seems at least right now it was very meaningful to you."

"It is somehow very different than the typical one-night stand. Just thinking about it makes me feel kind of gooey inside. Maybe tomorrow, I'll have a different feeling about it, but right now it makes me happy."

"That's good. You deserve to be happy."

"Well, I've heard you *'catting'* around here with different people. I didn't think you should have all the fun. The thing that gets me with you though is that many of them were young men. How can you do that? Just the thought of me making love with another woman makes my stomach turn. I just couldn't do it."

"Just because I bring someone home with me doesn't mean they are here for sex. Anyway, you just made love with a sweet young man, so why can't I?

"It just doesn't seem right, that's all. The parts don't fit."

"The way I look at it is that it's the pleasure you're seeking in any relationship, and that can be delivered by many different means. As I've said before, the external genitalia should not determine whom you are attracted to. You just want that certain vibration in your loins, which sends a message to the pleasure centers in your brain, which gives you that overpowering sensation of pleasure. Why does it matter how it was achieved?"

"I just can't believe I would feel that with another woman. And besides, I know that special feeling is much more powerful when I reach that special moment at the same time as my partner does. The pleasure is enhanced by the knowledge that you have brought pleasure to your partner. It's an extra special feeling when the pleasure is shared with someone you love."

"Well, you've got me there, love. When you don't know or like your love partner, there is something missing. That's why I'll sometimes send someone who doesn't measure up home and make love to myself. At least I know I'm having sex with someone I love."

"Now, that's something I don't want to talk about. Besides, you're just playing with words, you, big poop."

"Yes, you're right. People don't like to talk about that. Which brings me to Henry."

"How did Henry get into this?"

"Well, I would prefer if you don't tell him what you did today. He has become very fond of you and it might make him feel bad."

"I sensed something the other night but he has never said anything."

"When he threw himself over you to keep the bullets away the other day, it told me a lot. It wasn't me he first thought of to protect, it was you, even though you had been giving him a hard time since the first time you met."

"Oh, fiddle. We're all friends. I am very fond of both of you."

"And your young lover today?"

"Once in a lifetime. It won't happen again. I'm off to bed… night."

"Wait a minute. While you were having fun with the move, Dad and I made a couple of more contacts. So, that makes about a dozen so far that have received our request for proposal. Another guy wants to talk with us personally tomorrow. Do you think you will be up to it?"

"Sure, I'm ready to go. Is that it?"

"Yeah, that's it. Sleep tight, you, little vixen."

CHAPTER SIX

Dani slept late, and when she entered the study on the way to the kitchen for a wake up cup of coffee, she found Jonathan and Henry hunched over the computer studying the screen intently. They were talking to the security chief and information technology officer. "What's going on guys?"

No one acknowledged her until she poked Jonathan on the shoulder and said, "Hey, hello. It's me.”

“Yes. Hi, sweetheart. Someone is attacking our computer system and Steve is attempting to block it. Right now, it’s touch and go, but we seem to be just a step ahead of them. We’re not sure how long we can hold out without shutting down.”

“But all the real sensitive stuff is not in the cloud, so what’s the big deal?”

“Nobody is going to break into my goddamned system without my permission,” Jonathan ranted. “When I find out who the son of a bitch is, I’ll crush his nuts with a hammer and laugh while he bleeds to death.”

“Jeez, isn’t that a bit extreme, even for you, Jonathan?”

“This is personal, god dammit. Steve, how is it coming? I can send Dani down if you need another pair of hands."

"It's a pretty sophisticated attack. But so far, our defenses are holding. I'll let you know if I need more help."

"Just turn the mirror program on. It will throw everything back and hopefully, crash their system," Dani suggested.

"Yeah, he did that, and he could see the smoke fly a couple of times," Jonathan smiled. "The thing that worried me most is that we are getting a lot of attention, and I'm not sure who they all are. They could all be bad guys, which is probably okay. If on the other hand Homeland Security is sniffing around, we may have to call the auction sooner than I would like."

"Maybe we should take some time right now to define exactly how the auction will be held and how the big blow will be delivered," Dani suggested.

"That would be a good idea, Jonathan. I have some ideas," Henry chimed in.

"Oh yeah? Like what?"

"Well, for one, we have only talked about the 'get-everyone-together-and-blow-the-bastards-up' option. But that would only take care of the people invited to the auction. What about the arms themselves and the people guarding them?" Henry questioned. "We need to eliminate them as well."

"Good point, Henry. I agree with you," Dani added. "And besides, we don't want to blow up a perfectly good building if we don't have to."

"Yeah, yeah. I hear what you're saying. Let each of us think about it a little more. Then, we can get together over a glass of port after the computer system attack has been put to bed. Don't forget we have to visit another potential bidder this afternoon." Jonathan then turned back to the computer and said, "Steve, are there any further questions or information I need?"

"No, I think we're up to date."

"Okay, I'm signing off. Keep me informed via call if necessary."

"Okay, chief."

Turning back to Dani and Henry, Jonathan said, "I don't know much about the guy we're supposed to see this afternoon. Let each of us see what we can find out about him on the web. We leave here at one thirty."

"Okay, Jony. But first, I have a poem for you Dani."

"Well you show me yours, and I'll show you mine."

"Now, that is definitely something to think about, but for now here's the poem;

> *There once was a pretty white cat,*
> *Who loved to curl up in a hat.*
> *His eyes were as blue as the sky,*
> *And as big as a blueberry pie.*
> *But when confronted by a rat,*
> *The pretty white kitty would scat.*

There's mine, said Henry. Now show me yours.

"Okay, that's a toughie but here goes:

> *There once was a man from Tennessee,*
> *Who when walking in the woods had to pee.*
> *But his member was unusually small,*
> *Though he searched he could not find it at all*
> *So down came his pants and he watered a nearby tree."*

"Ha, ha! I love it. Not too shabby. This is fun." Henry opined.

"I agree, but I've got to have something to eat,"

Dani replied.

"I'll join you, little glutton. I wish I could eat like you and keep my weight down" Henry replied.

"All you have to do is exercise every day like I do. You should come and work out with me in the mornings."

"That's a swimming idea, my dear. Now, take my hand and help this old geezer to the kitchen."

After a leisurely brunch and some time on the computer, Jonathan and his entourage descended in the elevator and made their way across the lobby. A bellboy who handed an envelope to Dani interrupted them. On the face of the envelope was scrolled, *'To Dani from Roger: Urgent please open now!'*

After reading the envelope, Dani said, "Hold on guys. This could be important." *Or it could be embarrassing* Dani thought as she ripped open the envelope. It read; *'Dani the meeting you are off to right now is a trap. Please meet me in Conference Room A, and let me explain. I am serious. If you go to the meeting, your life will be in danger!!! I need to talk to you now!!! Come alone. Roger'*

"Jonathan, this could be important. It's about the meeting we are off to. I need to look into it before we leave."

"Oh, for god's sake, Dani. We are a little late leaving already."

"The message is from Roger. He says it's a matter of life or death. I have at least got to check it out. It should only take a minute or two."

"If this has something to do with your moving day experience, I'm going to shoot you. Go ahead, and check it out while we get the limo ready. But I'm warning you, this better be important!"

"Hey, I'm as annoyed as you are, but I at least have to check it out. I'll meet you out front."

Roger was sitting in a chair with his back to the door as Dani entered Conference Room A. His jacket collar was pulled up and his baseball cap was pulled down to almost completely covering his face. As Dani approached him, she said, "Roger is that you?"

"Yes, Dani, it's me. I'm taking a big chance here. I hope I don't get us both killed."

"You sound scared Roger. What is this all about?"

"You can't say anything about me to your people or about what I have to tell you."

"Oh, come on. Just because we had wonderful sex together is not a life or death thing."

"It doesn't have anything to do with that. The meeting you're going to is a trap, and it could lead to a shootout."

"What are you talking about? How do you know about the meeting anyway?"

"I have been associated with that group for some time. I had to fake a brief move to get here without them knowing."

"Why would they want to kill a potential buyer? That doesn't make much sense."

"That's the point. They are not sellers. They are buyers just like you, and they want to get rid of competition."

"How are you privy to all this information? You work for a moving company?"

"That's just one of their fronts. They were

doing just fine until you guys poked your nose in. The prices started to rise because of the added demand. Manny doesn't like competition, and he is a very ruthless guy."

"I'm having trouble getting my head around this. Are you really an arms dealer or a mover?"

"I'm both, technically speaking."

"Manny wants to wipe out his competition so he can make more money?"

"Yes. That's it in a nutshell."

"Come out, and tell your story to Jonathan."

"I can't expose myself anymore than I have. If they discover that I'm here talking to you, both of us are as good as dead."

"If you are one of them, why are you warning us not to go there?"

"Mainly because I don't want you to get hurt."

"That's sweet, but it's also the dumbest thing I've ever heard of."

"Well, I agree. It sounds dumb. I can hardly believe I'm here."

"Well, at least we agree on one thing. Now, what do we do?"

"As I see it, you have two options. You just go there as if you didn't know anything about the trap and try to shoot it out with them, or you could drive there and wait in the car for a while and then leave without going in. I honestly don't know which would be best. At least the second option may buy you some time."

"I've got to talk to Jonathan about this. Hold on while I get him on the cell." While Dani was preoccupied with the phone and explaining everything to Jonathan, Roger slipped out of the room. When Dani discovered he was gone, she ran to the door and looked in the lobby for him all the while on the phone with Jonathan. When Roger was nowhere to be found, she proceeded to the limo.

"Blimey! That's a wild story," Jonathan said when Dani reached the limo. "We need more time to check out this Roger guy to determine the veracity of his story as well as how to best proceed. Steve did a preliminary search and found someone with that name working at Manny's Movers. I guess that could be him but we're not actually sure of that. He doesn't seem to have a history before he got that job and that's kind of strange."

"Well, I tend to believe him," Dani interjected. "I don't think we can just barge in there not knowing what to expect in terms of fire power and strategy, so that option is out for me."

"I trust Dani's instincts," Henry added. "With the second option, they may think that something at the house may have spooked us, and will try to reschedule, giving us some time to plan our next move."

"Logic tells me that we should proceed as if the warning is true until it's proven otherwise. So, I think the simplest thing to do is just call Manny and cancel the meeting."

"I like that idea," Dani broke in. "You could say you are sick with a contagious disease and try to reschedule for a week or so. That would give us time to check out Roger and maybe I could find and talk to him further."

"If what he says is true, that could put you both in danger just as he said," Jonathan railed. "God damn it, Dani! I don't know whether to kiss you or spank your butt. What do you think pops?"

"I think we should proceed with the phone call. That's the simplest and safest approach."

"Okay, here we go." Jonathan dialed.

After passing through several people, Manny growled into the phone. "Where the fuck are you, Broxton? We are supposed to be meeting right now."

"Hello, Manny. Best regards to you also. I am sorry for the late call but my doctor has vetoed the visit. Seems I'm very contagious right now and I wouldn't want to give the bug to you. So, I was thinking that we could meet next week or I could send a courier over with the materials. They are self-explanatory and it might speed things up. What do you think?"

"I think that's bullshit! Get your ass over here right now or there will be no deal."

"Well, if that's the way you want it, that's fine

with me. I have plenty of people interested in the auction. So, I guess the deal is off. Goodbye."

"Wait a minute, you, son of a bitch. Send the fucking materials. I'll decide what I want to do with them." He slammed the phone down, terminating the conversation.

Jonathan turned to his cohorts and said sarcastically, "I think that went pretty well. There were a few words that could have been left out, but we got what we wanted. Now, let's find out everything we can about Roger and make preparations for the auction. Things have become too visible to continue soliciting more bidders."

Henry looked a little bewildered and asked, "Who the hell is this Roger guy, and how do you know him, Dani?"

Dani stole a glance at Jonathan before

answering, recalling Jonathan's admonition not to tell Henry what really happened on moving day. "He was the guy in charge of the move from my apartment to the hotel."

"That's it? And now he's risking his neck to save yours? I think there's more to this story than you're saying."

"We don't have time to go into that right now. Who knows what motivates people to do unusual things?"

"We could see if there is a match to any of the faces in facial recognition profiles," Dani blurted out. "I think Steve has access to all the local law enforcement files as well as FBI, CIA and Homeland security."

"That's all well and good if we had a good picture of him. You said he had camouflaged himself so much that the security tapes here wouldn't show us anything. Is that right?"

"Yeah, I think so."

"Hell! Maybe it wasn't even the same guy," Henry suggested.

"It was him alright," Dani said with certainty. Then remembering Jonathan's admonition not to tell Henry about her dalliance with Roger, she added, "Jonathan, can I have a word with you please?"

As they moved out of Henry's earshot, he said, "Hey, what's going on here? What aren't you guys telling me?"

"Dani whispered to Jonathan, "I secretly took some pictures of Roger on my cell. I think they will work. And maybe, I could find a fingerprint on some of my furniture."

"Damn, Dani. You are going to drive me crazy with your antics. But this time, I think I should kiss you. This could be just the break we need. Get your fanny up to Steve and see what can be done."

Dani shouted back as she left the room, "Got it, chief. See you guys upstairs."

Jonathan then turned to Henry, "Let's get upstairs and start planning our next move."

"I'm not going anywhere until you let me in on that little secret you and Dani are keeping from me."

"Hey, it's a minor thing that didn't involve you. I'll tell you everything when we get upstairs. Come on."

CHAPTER SEVEN

"Here's the deal," Jonathan said after he and Henry were in the study sitting comfortably, each with a freshly opened glass of Graham's 1945 Vintage Port.

After taking a small sip, Henry sat back in his chair and swirled the libation around his mouth and slowly swallowed. He paused and said, "Damn, Jonathan. This is great stuff. Where did you get it?"

"It was a gift from my best friend about ten years ago."

"Oh, really? Who is that?"

"You." Jonathan smiled.

"I don't remember that. Jeez, I do have good taste."

"It was for my big 30. At the time, I thought life, as I knew it, was all over. We sat and talked over a bottle and you gave me another as a gift to be drunk at a later date of my choosing. This is it."

"What's so special about today?"

"Dani thinks she may have a usable picture or finger print of Roger."

"And that helps us how?"

"Once we determine who he is, we will know if

he is a threat or not."

"He seems to have helped us this time."

"Yeah, but we don't know how to proceed until we know what his game is."

"Guess that makes sense. How did she get the pictures?"

"She secretly took the pictures during the move, and he may have left a print or two on some of her furniture."

"Well, I'll be damned. Does she have a crush on him or what?"

"Not really. I think she just liked the muscles."

"And that's the secret between you two?"

"See, I told you it was a minor thing."

Jonathan paused for a moment to let Henry deal with Dani's picture taking, and hoping no further questions would have to be answered. He then continued, "Anyway, let's try to get some clarity about exactly how the end game will be played."

"Dani's just a kid. She does kid things," Henry observed.

"We started a discussion earlier today about the wisdom of blowing everyone up after bringing them together for the auction. You had some opinions. Care to elaborate?"

"The more I thought about it the dumber the idea sounded. First of all, we want to do away with more than just the bad guys, and second, why destroy a perfectly good meeting place?"

"We could meet at one of their locations which contain the weapons," Jonathan interrupted.

Henry ignored Jonathan's last point and said, "Besides, how do we blow them up without blowing ourselves up? There's got to be a better way."

"Those are all good points, Pops. There's got to be a better way. One thing we could do is use a toxic chemical or poison such as Risin."

"Yes, but that leaves the weapons and our safety."

"How about visiting each of the facilities prior to the auction to inspect them? While there, we could leave some explosives of our own with a remote controlled trigger. That way, at the appropriate time, we could detonate everyone's stores at the same time."

"All good points. On the face of it, the last one sounds good but man, would it be risky. We'll have to run all this by Dani when she finishes her Miss

Marple routine. In the meantime, pour me another glass of Port you got from your very best friend."

"I know you're kidding me a little, but you know it's true. You are my father and that relationship is very special to me."

"Yes, I know. I feel the same way."

"I can relate to you more than a confidante, more as a best friend. I can tell you what's on my mind and know you will accept it without reservation and give feedback that is always right on the mark. I feel particularly blessed." Jonathan raised his glass in salutation and said, "Here's to my father and best friend."

He tried to hide it but as Henry's hand rose tears filled his eyes and he was barely able to whisper, "Here, here."

There followed a long winding discussion of right and wrong, life and death, and the existence of a higher Being. And of course, they consumed the entire contents of the Graham 1945 Vintage Port, so warmly given those many years ago.

This glorious interlude was totally shattered by Dani bursting into the room shouting, "I got him! I got him! I finally know who Roger really is!" She stood there waving several pages of paper expecting an ovation and an exalted response to her announcement. Instead, she was virtually ignored by these wise old guys, too dense to appreciate her wondrous accomplishment.

"Damn it, you guys! Did you hear what I said? Do you understand what this means?"

At which point, Jonathan slowly responded, "Oh! Hi, Dani. Where have you been?"

Dani stamped her foot angrily and surveyed the scene. She soon recognized the meaning of the enormously under-appreciated revelation she had delivered, and shouted to no one in particular, "He's one of us, dammit…. he's one of us!" and then sat down on the nearest chair and cried into her hands until she fell asleep.

CHAPTER EIGHT

Dani had fallen asleep on the couch in the living room with the boys after stating that Roger was one of them. She was shaken awake in the morning by Jonathan saying, "Do I remember right that someone was one of us? What the hell did you mean by that?"

Dani slowly opened her eyes and replied, "Roger is one of us, of course. What do you think I was working on all day yesterday?"

"Oh yeah, Roger. What did you mean he was one of us?"

"Well, I exhausted all the databases we have access to with no luck. So then, I started calling all my old friends in the CIA. One of them remembered him. He had gone undercover a couple of years ago and hadn't heard from him since. Roger was his undercover name. That explains why I wasn't able to find the name in any of the databases. It's got to be the same guy."

"Maybe, but we need more proof than that before we get more familiar with him. However, it does sound promising. I made some coffee. do you want some?"

"Of course. And while I'm refreshing myself, here's another limerick:

I like to sit and make a rhyme,
It's really not a waste of time.
It helps to stimulate my brain,
And keep it from circling down the drain.
But I must finish them while I'm in my prime."

After reciting her limerick, she sat back with a very satisfied look on her face.

"Not bad, but I have one that's just a little bit better," Henry exclaimed.

My mental synapses have withered with age,
Extraneous debris has put my mind in a cage.
But the message usually gets through,
Maybe a little past it's timely due.
And the quality of thought remains just as sage."

Then Henry waited for a response.

"That was very introspective but I'm not so sure that it's better than mine. I'd be happy to discuss it further, but I've got to take a shower. I think I'm a bit ripe."

At which point Henry piped up, "Oh, good.

Can I watch?"

"You are such a dirty old man," Dani laughed. "I'm going to lock the door to make sure that doesn't happen."

After they all finished their coffee, Dani said, "Well, I'm off for my shower."

Henry said, "Wait for me."

But Dani quickly raced to the door and closed it before Henry could get there as Henry muttered, "Ah, come on! Give an old geezer a break."

"The door is locked and you can't come in," Dani giggled.

"I'm dying of anticipation. My death will be on your hands."

"I'll tell you what, as I get undressed, I'll tell you what item of clothing I'm taking off. Then, you can use your imagination. That's probably better than the real thing anyway, don't you think?"

"Dani, please I'm dying out here," Henry laughed.

Jonathan chimed in, "You, kids. Play nice now."

"I'm unbuttoning my blouse and dropping it on the floor," Dani announced. "And oops! There goes the skirt. Oh my, I'm standing here in my bra and panties."

Henry let out a groan and banged on the door. "Dani, I love you."

"Yeah! You would lie just to get in here, wouldn't you... oops! There goes the bra and panties. I'm standing here, bare naked with my back toward you. And now, I'm bending over at the waist to pick up my panties."

"Oh, god! Dani, you are so beautiful. I'm growing bananas out here!"

"Good. Now, I'm turning around facing you and wiggling my boobies. Oh my, what am I going to do next?"

"I'll show you what to do, just open this damn door. Watching you through this key hole just doesn't cut it."

"What...what keyhole?" She had forgotten that this was an old hotel, and although they added new locks, they did not tamper with the old keyhole in order to keep the authenticity of the place intact as much as possible. For a moment, she was stunned, but then scampered over to the door, found the keyhole and looked out only to find Henry looking back.

She screamed, "Henry, I hate you!" Then, she

hung her panties over the doorknob and ran for the bathroom.

"Dani, you sure put on a beautiful show."

After listening to the give and take between Henry and Dani, Jonathan with a broad smile repeated, "You almost got what you wanted dad, and maybe all that you could handle."

Things finally turned back to normal after about an hour. Dani, with a sheepish look on her face, returned to the living room without looking at Henry. She silently prepared her breakfast and sat down to eat before Henry spoke to her. "I'm sorry, sweetheart. I was a cad. Please forgive me."

"I don't know, Henry. I am very embarrassed. I should have acted more maturely. It's not all your fault. Tell me, you don't remember anything you saw, and maybe we can put it all behind us."

"Okay. I don't remember a thing. But you did put on a beautiful show."

Dani quickly got up and ran to Henry and started to playfully pound him with her hands until Henry yelled, "I give up. I didn't see anything, okay?"

She continued to pound away until her cell phone beeped telling her she had a text message. She said, "I'm not done with you yet, Henry, but this could be important." She flipped her phone open and it read, *Dani, I need to see you. Very important. Come to 217 North Street. You must come alone. I will meet you. Please don't let me down. Roger.*

"Roger is in trouble. What do you think I should do, Jonathan?"

"He seems like he could be important to us, so I think you should go. We will fit you with a GPS device, so we know exactly where you are and we will follow at a safe distance. We can fit you with an ultra-small, two-way earpiece, so we can stay in touch. Just say *'things are rosy'* and our team will be there in minutes. But it's your decision, what do you want to do?"

"I've got to go. I have no choice. Get the stuff, and get me out of here."

Dani pulled to a stop at 217 North Street and said, "Okay, guys. Here goes. Everything looks peaceful."

Henry chipped in, "You be careful, sweetheart. Signal us at the slightest provocation."

She exited her car, gun in hand, and approached a van parked at the curb. It appeared to be empty. As she turned and started for the building, someone shot her with a stun gun and she fell almost immediately to the ground. The charge was so intense that it knocked out both the GPS and the earpiece. Someone picked her up, dragged her to the van and sped off before her team knew anything was wrong.

When communications were lost, the team sped to the address, but when they got there they could see no one. They proceeded to the front door and kicked it in only to find a very frightened old lady and her blind dog. They had completely lost contact with Dani.

In the van, someone tied her feet and hands, placed duct tape over her mouth and put a hood over her head. She slowly recovered from the taser shot, but was unable to discern in which direction the van was traveling, or how far they were from the original address.

After driving for some time, the van stopped

and Dani heard what she thought was a garage door opening, and the van pulled in and the door shut. She lay alone on the floor of the van until the side door opened and someone put his meaty hands under her arms and pulled her to the door. He then stood her up and put his shoulder into her stomach and lifted her onto his shoulder like a sack of flour. He didn't even grunt. He must have been a big strong guy.

He walked away with her over his shoulder, through two doors and down a flight of stairs. She surmised that she was in the basement of some building but she had no idea what the address was. For all she knew, she could be right back where she started. He deposited her on the cold concrete floor and left. She was bound hand and foot, duct tape over her mouth and the hood still over her head. She assumed she was alone and lay quietly for some time as she gathered her strength and her thoughts.

After several minutes her reverie was broken by a muffled cough or sneeze. She was not alone. Because she didn't know if her unknown companion was friend or foe, she lay quiet until she couldn't take it any further. She then made as much noise as she could and began struggling with her bindings. Shortly, she heard the same type of commotion from across the room. She thought *I'm here with a friend. Could it be Roger?*

The thought that she was with another bound person caused her to struggle even more. She finally raised herself to her feet by sitting against the wall and pressing while pushing with her feet and wiggling her backside. She slid up and down, hoping the hood would catch on something and pull it off. After struggling for some time, off came the hood and she fell back to the floor. She could now see her companion but of course could not determine who it was because he or she was bound and gagged just like she was.

After surveying her surroundings for some time, she laid on her side and began to make snake-like movements and inched her way toward her struggling fellow prisoner. Upon reaching the bound person, she worked herself to her knees and felt for the hood. She was able to work her way up the wall while holding the edge of the hood and was eventually able to work it off. She then saw that it was indeed Rodger, and he, of course, recognized her.

They each began to rub the duct tape that covered their mouths against their shoulder to loosen it. Then, she raised herself to her knees, turned with her back toward him and was finally able to remove the tape over his mouth with the fingers of her bound hands. "Dani, am I ever glad to see you. Please forgive me for getting you into this mess." As he spoke, he followed Dani's example and finally removed the tape over her mouth.

Gasping and spitting, Dani muttered, "God, that feels good." And after a pause, she examined his face and let out a whistle, "My god, what have they done to your face?"

"I don't know what it looks like but they beat me up pretty good." There were several gashes oozing blood along with his nose and mouth.

Both eyes were black and swollen, and she had trouble making out his beautiful features. She could barely keep from crying. In sympathy, she bent over and rubbed his cheek with hers. His only response was, "Ouch."

"Why did you send that text message?"

"What text message?"

"The one that got me captured. You said you were in deep trouble and asked me to come bail you out."

"I didn't send any message. His people must have done that. Apparently, they had followed me the day I came to your hotel, cause shortly after that, I found myself down here, and someone was beating on me."

"Who are we talking about?"

"The arms dealer I was working for."

"What did you tell them?"

"Nothing."

"I found out that you were an undercover CIA agent."

"Oh you did, did you?"

"Do you deny it?"

"Shush! Somebody may be listening."

"We'll have to talk about that later. See if you can get the barrette from my hair, and give it to me."

Roger followed her instructions, and when she got the barrette, she pushed the back until it exposed a small razor blade, and she began to work on the rope that bound Roger's hands. Once free, Roger untied Dani and they sat back and began plotting their next move.

They knew that people had to come down the stairs eventually. Roger suggested if the two of them could arrange ropes strategically and pull them, Taute at the right time, it could trip the bad guys and make them fall down the stairs. While they were incapacitated, Roger and Dani could overcome them.

They could then bind the bad guys just as they had been bound. They would then be armed with the weapons taken from their captors and they could try to sneak or fight their way out of the place.

There were two small windows that were large enough for them to get through, but had bars covering them which would be hard to remove. Whatever they did would have to be done quickly because someone was probably waiting for them upstairs, and they would soon come looking for their compatriots.

The correct action was clear, and they began the placement of the ropes. They didn't have to wait long before the door opened and two men began to descend the stairs. Both Dani and Roger were in position as their captors came down the stairs. At just the right instant, they pulled the ropes. The second captor tripped first and as he fell into the first, the second rope was pulled and both captors fell in a heap at the foot of the stairs. Roger grabbed the top guy and threw him against the concrete wall and beat on him until he was unconscious. He then began to tape his mouth and tie his hands and feet with the ropes which he removed from the stairs.

Dani pounced on her man, and even though he attempted to strike her, she was finally able to place him into a sleeper hold. Even though he slammed her against the walls, the floor, and posts, she was able to maintain the pressure until he was unconscious. Though she was cut and bruised, and in pain, she bound and gagged her victim.

When both victims were secured, Dani and Roger collected their weapons and bullet clips, and quietly made their way up the stairs where the door had been left ajar. Peering into the room, they could see going right would take them into another room of the house, but they heard voices from there. There was a closed door on the left which they chose as a safer bet. They quietly stole across the kitchen and listened for an instant, hearing nothing. They opened the door which led them into the garage where there were two cars. They both had learned breaking and entering techniques as CIA agents. They quickly wired the car and Roger started the engine, placed the gearshift in reverse and stepped hard on the accelerator. The wheels screeched and the car broke through the door with a thunderous roar. Only then could they see the driveway and the street. They were thankful that no car was parked in the driveway.

Once in the street, they sped away. They kept driving until Roger recognized where they were and quickly sped toward the hotel from there. They parked the stolen car in the hotel garage and made their way to the penthouse where Jonathan and Henry welcomed them home.

CHAPTER NINE

Jonathan, upon seeing Roger, gasped and said, "My god, man. They really did a number on your face!"

"My boss's thugs beat me up pretty good. I think he had me followed when I came to warn you about your meeting with him last week."

"You are too gruesome to look at the way you are, so come with me to the bathroom." On the way, Jonathan said, "You can take a shower and clean up.

I'll lay out some first aid stuff and a change of clothes."

"That would be great. When I get out, I imagine we have a lot to talk about."

"You can say that again. In the meantime, Dani, can you bring us up to speed?"

"I won't be too long," Roger promised as he left the room.

When Roger was gone, Jonathan turned to Dani and said, "What happened out there?"

Dani spared no detail in recounting her captivity and escape, and then said, "As far as Roger's name, assignment, allegiances etc., that's still uncertain. But I believe he is an undercover CIA agent just as my friend said. He almost said as much when we were planning our escape."

"Well, that's something we have to be certain of before we get very deep in our plans. The next is, where do we fit into CIA's plans, and what can he do about it. Once all that's cleared up to our satisfaction, we can make our final plans and determine where he fits in, or if he does at all."

Jonathan set about preparing for the discussion with Roger, while Henry scowled in disbelief. He regarded Roger as a competitor for Dani's affections and wasn't about to accept his word for anything. Reluctantly, he opened the bottle of wine that Jonathan set out and sat down to wait for Roger to prove who he was.

The three colleagues were sitting around the coffee table, nibbling cheese and crackers, and sipping a nicely aged Claret when Rodger came back. He was much more presentable and clean, but was festooned with small band aids and other sealed off scrapes. His eyes were black and blue.

"Thank you for the change of clothes. They are a perfect fit. I don't know how you did it, but I appreciate it. Now, where do we begin?"

As Jonathan poured Roger a glass of wine, he said, "We start by you telling us exactly who the hell you are."

"Fair enough." He cleared his throat and then continued, "I have learned enough about you guys that I'm convinced you are not a typical weapons dealer. I have not been able to determine what you are up to, but I think it can't be all bad."

"Yeah, yeah. Just get to the point. Who the hell are you, and why shouldn't we just put a bullet in you? It would be a lot quicker," Henry ungraciously blurted out.

"You seem to be very hostile, Henry, and I

can't blame you for that. But if you will give me a few minutes, I think I can convince you that I mean you no harm."

Sheepishly, Henry said, "Yeah, well, just get on with it."

"It's totally against protocol, but I think I better come clean. Yes, I am with the CIA."

"How do we know that's the truth?" Henry wanted to know.

"First of all, the person that Dani talked to about me had the authority to contact me, and he filled me in about things I didn't know. He confirmed that you're not out to threaten national security. He also said that you seemed to be trying to accomplish the same thing we are. He just didn't know how and when."

Jonathan interrupted, "That's very interesting.

So, what does the CIA intend to do with us and when?"

"For now, just watch and wait. But we'd be prepared to pounce quickly."

"Is the CIA close to acting against the arms dealers that we have been in contact with?"

"If there is enough evidence to win a legal case against both the bad guys and you, we'd turn it over to the FBI. They would need to act soon before any more arms flow to our enemies."

"You've got to persuade them that we are close to completing our plan to eliminate that from happening," Jonathan implored. "And that our actions would yield more of a sure thing than going to trial."

"I can only do that if I know what your plans are. Show me yours, and I'll show you mine."

"Before we go any further, I want Dani to speak to her CIA contact, and confirm what you have said. I hope her contact is legitimate and has the authority to throttle down action until he hears the details of our plan."

"He's very close to the top, so if he like your plan, then we can carry it out. That's fair enough."

"Our plans are a little unconventional, so the CIA will have to be on board. We are prepared to take the heat if something goes wrong."

"We can make the proposal and see where it leads, okay?"

"As you say, fair enough," Jonathan said while examining Roger's demeanor very closely. "Dani, please go do your thing, and get back to us as soon as possible."

Within minutes, Dani had her CIA commander on a secure phone line. He said, he personally knew Roger and had full authority to obtain and present to him the plan. He then requested to talk personally with Roger, and Dani handed him the phone. The two of them talked for several minutes before Roger hung up.

"He confirmed that the CIA was close to raiding the facilities of the weapons dealers they were aware of and confiscating any weapons found. That makes it important that we act swiftly."

"In a nutshell, our plan is to destroy the weapons that have been assembled at our behest, along with as many of the responsible people that we can lure to the sight."

"And how do you intend to do that exactly?"

"We prepared a detailed list of the weapons

we wanted to buy and distributed it to all the dealers we discovered. Then, several more contacted us to get in on the auction our brochure outlined. We included only those who would consent to an inspection of their weapons by one of our agents. Once the list is finalized, our plan is to plant in their C-4, a timing device which when activated would cause the C-4 to explode and take the rest of the ammunition in the warehouse with it. The amount that we specified is large enough to level an entire warehouse."

"And what about the leaders?"

"All bidders will submit their lowest price at a specified time. They must be at their warehouse to receive payment because we would be there immediately upon notification to load and transport the weapons. At the instant of notification, every bidders' C-4 will be exploded at the same time killing everyone at or near every warehouse."

"Geez, that is pretty extreme. How the hell would you pull that off?"

"I've had our scientific guys working with a combination of Nano technology and C-4. Their charge is to create a rope consisting of natural fibers combined with Nano strands of C-4, in such a way that it looks just like a normal rope," Jonathan explained.

"That would be quite a breakthrough," Roger said.

"After the rope is manufactured, the idea is to arrange a time to visit each site. The purpose of the visit is to confirm that they had all-- or substantially all-- of the weapons we asked for, especially the C-4. We tell them that the C-4 is essential. To ensure that the stuff has not been tampered with between the time of the inspection and the time we pick it up after the final bid is accepted, we will wrap it with our magic rope and seal it. We tell them that if the seal is broken when we come to pick it up, all bets are off. Now, what they don't know is that the seal is a radio transceiver which when the correct signal is sent, starts the C-4 fiber to vibrate at a rate that heats them up. When the fibers reach a certain temperature, they explode. This, in turn, will cause the entire stash of C-4 to explode. When the C-4 explodes, it will destroy everything in the warehouse including the bad guys. One signal will set off all of the C-4 in all of the locations we have visited at the same time. Mission accomplished." Jonathan said proudly.

"After the explosions, the CIA can conduct a thorough investigation and come out smelling like a rose when they determine that the whole thing was a turf war gone bad. As I have been speaking, my words have been transcribed and with a little editing will be ready for you to take to your leader."

"Man, that's an outrageous plan. The CIA would never approve it officially, even though it does meet the overall goals. Too controversial," Roger responded.

"We don't have to tell them. We don't need their help to pull this off."

"Yes, you're right. We don't have to tell them everything. However, we would have to carry it out without their backup. Are you sure we can do that?"

"That's what I had in mind all along. If they are involved, too many things can go wrong. We don't need their help, except perhaps to stay out of our hair until the job is done," Jonathan assured.

"Okay. I can keep them from doing anything until after the investigation. But we have to be sure that they can't trace the explosion back to the CIA. Otherwise, all of our asses will be in deep trouble," Roger said.

Henry chimed in, "You sure say 'us' a lot, but you're not part of this team."

"Well maybe, not officially, but I'm in this now up to my eyeballs. If this fails, my career is over. If you let me, I'm with you one hundred percent. Just tell me what you want me to do."

CHAPTER TEN

All the team members assembled in the lobby of the St. Pierre, in preparation for yet another inspection of the arms dealers participating in the auction. They divided into two teams as usual, so that the site inspections and weapons securing could be done as quickly as possible. The limos were loaded with the magic rope, transceivers blanket, and all the tools needed to look like they knew what they were doing.

Walt would drive the limo for Roger and Henry, and Bob would drive the limo for Dani and Jonathan. Everyone was delighted that the end of their project was at hand.

Jonathan barked out the orders as usual, "Okay, guys. I know you know what to do by now, so I'll just say good luck. Be damned careful out there! We've been very lucky so far, and I'm anxious to get this over with while luck is still with us." Then he continued with an optimistic note, "But on the other hand, how could it be any other way? The good guys always win, right?"

Henry added, "We're all pepped up. Let's get going before I start singing *'God Bless America'*."

Before they could leave, Dani interjected, "In that vain, I have a limerick for your pleasure:

There once was a man from Connecticut
Who was profoundly lacking in etiquette.
He offered his hand when he should have bowed,
And he spoke too much and too loud.
But worst of all, he frequently misplaced a
predicate."

Henry responded, "That's not bad, but a little too academic for this situation. I think I have one that fits the present situation a little better:

There once was a man from Boston,
Whose full name was Jonathan Broxton.
His wisdom and money were renowned.
So he sought respect more profound.
Now he is the terrorist's public enemy number
one."

"That one certainly hits the nail on the head, but I like them both. Thanks for the Plebeian humor," Jonathan replied, then added, "Good luck everyone."

The limo carrying Roger and Henry proceeded in silence toward their destination. After about twenty minutes, Bob announced that they had arrived. Henry surveyed the location with fascination, "Jeez! This is just a row of brownstones. How are they going to house all of the weapons here?"

Surprised, he and Roger nevertheless proceeded to the front door with their bag of goodies. Henry pressed the doorbell and a voice asked over a speaker, "Please state your name and business for being here."

Henry stated his name, the agreed upon password and the purpose of his visit, at which point the voice demanded, "Each person in turn look into the camera until the red light flashes, then place your right palm on the glass below the camera until the light goes out." After they complied with the instructions the voice said, "Stand by for further instructions."

After a brief delay, the door buzzed, automatically opened, and the *voice* instructed them, "Move forward and conduct your inspection as soon as possible, and leave the building the way you entered. Your movements will be strictly monitored. Suspicious behavior will not be tolerated."

Surprised by the lack of personal supervision, Henry and Roger nevertheless felt the heavy hand of big brother, and had the feeling that any false move would be dealt with swiftly and harshly. With much foreboding, they opened their duffel bag and with clipboard in hand began the methodical identification of all the weaponry and checked it off. When they came to the C-4, they ran a test to determine its quality, and after they were satisfied, they began to wrap the pallet with the magic rope. The *voice* demanded, "Stop what you are doing until the rope can be examined, and you are given instructions to proceed."

At that point, Roger opened the bag completely and held it up for inspection, while Henry did the same with the rope. Not knowing where the inspection would come from, they slowly turned around in a circle at which point the *voice* demanded, "Do not move while our inspection proceeds." In due course, the voice again announced, "You may proceed."

After completing the wrapping, Henry began to apply the transceiver blanket which unknown to the *voice* was also the detonator. The *voice* once again demanded, "Stop what you are doing until that material is examined." Henry explained that the material was simply a wax like seal, so that he could determine if the wrapped cargo had been tampered with before it was picked up after the auction.

He then heard a door open, and a small robot proceeded in their direction. The *voice* said, "Place the material on the robot's screen and wait for further instructions." After several agonizing moments, the *voice* said, "Proceed with your actions."

Much relieved, the pair proceeded with the installation, and when they finished, Henry announced to no one in particular but in the general direction of the voice, "We have finished our inspection and are satisfied that you have substantially met the requirements of the RFP. Your final bid must be registered on our website by exactly 1PM on Wednesday, with assurance that if your bid is chosen, that the person who signed the proposal, and can authorize payment into your account, is on the premises upon our arrival, no more than 15 minutes subsequent to notification of winning. If the person who submitted the proposal is not personally present upon our arrival, you will be disqualified and we will proceed to the next lowest bidder. Do you understand and agree to abide by these rules?"

After several minutes, the voice announced that the requirements were acceptable and that the inspectors were to vacate the premises immediately. They followed those instructions without hesitation, delighter to be free of the pressure exerted by the unseen monitoring and the *voice.* They now understood that an unseen threat is often more severely felt than that seen because it is impossible to prepare an adequate defense if necessary.

****

Meanwhile, Dani and Jonathan were piloted by Walt to their destination. In transit, Dani said to Jonathan, "I think that Roger and Henry make a good team. I was worried at first because of their crazy rivalry, but it worked out. I guess I shouldn't have been surprised because it took me a while to warm to Henry as well. Now, I can't, for the life of me, see why everyone doesn't just love the guy from day one."

"I think people sell dad short because he's an old guy. Age doesn't have the unquestioned respect in this country that it has in most other cultures. We pride ourselves in being a meritocracy, which requires competition to determine value and respect. Respect is bestowed only after someone has demonstrated their superior ability, and an old guy just isn't the first person to challenge for supremacy in a physical environment. In time, however, the benefit of experience and wisdom is valued more than strength and pompousness, and dad is nothing if not a very wise man. I think that's why in the end he wins people over."

"Well said, Jonathan." After a few minutes of silence Dani said, "Do you think we can finish up today?"

"If all goes well, today should be the end of inspections," Jonathan replied as Walt pulled to a stop in an area that was distinctly different from that confronted by their compatriots. They found themselves in the middle of the huge warehouse district.

What they saw reminded them of the WWII maximum security prisons; two concentric twenty-foot chain linked fences topped by intertwined rolls of razor wire. The area between the fences was packed with more electrified razor wire. There were several posted warnings about the danger of approaching the facility without prior authorization.

Anxiety streaked their faces as they approached the entrance gate where they were confronted by two heavily armed guards and their companion canines, all of which snarled their welcome, "State your name and the purpose for being here."

The visitors responded appropriately which was followed by grunts and silence, while all parties awaited the response from the higher ups. They could see five different security cameras trained on them, so they knew that not only was the information given but also their facial features and any number of other characteristics were scanned.

After what seemed to be a lifetime, the guards unchained the entrance gate and ushered the guests into a small holding cell where they underwent full body, eye, and palm scans. This was followed by another lapse of time before they were led down a hallway and into the warehouse where they were greeted by a very scantily dressed beautiful young woman.

They thought they must have made a wrong turn, and were about to turn around when the young woman said, "Good afternoon, people. I am Veronica. Allow me to examine the contents of your bag, and then you may continue with your examination of the warehouse's contents."

Veronica's blouse was definitely see-through and her tiny skirt barely covered the rope-thin thong that circled her lower body.

Dani silently stared at her costume and smiled in amusement. But upon closer examination, Veronica had well developed muscle groups in the calf and thigh, and further up the buttocks and abdominals were tight and showed no more than 10% body fat. Up further still, her breasts were slightly augmented but not extreme, and her shoulder and arm muscle groups were well developed and defined. This girl worked out a lot and seriously. Dani thought she would not like to be in hand-to-hand combat with the lady. Maybe she was more than a plaything, possibly a king maker, and she had to be taken seriously.

The young woman could see Dani's studied evaluation of her and walked slowly toward her. "What is your name," she demanded.

Dani stated her name and the young woman responded, "Yuck. I hate that name."

"It's short for Danielle," Dani explained through clenched teeth.

"It sounds like you're trying to be a dirty little boy," the young woman said and proceeded to poke Dani's arm with her finger.

"Thank you for sharing," Dani replied while yearning to place the young woman in an

Australian death grip.

"I don't like you. In the future, I will have to fight you," the young woman said as she stared at Dani with a pensive frown on her face and a stance that could at any moment become an attack. Dani stood her ground and tensed ready for an unwanted battle.

Feeling Dani's resolve, Veronica turned to Jonathan and smiled seductively before she proceeded to empty the bag's contents on the floor and rummaged through the items. She stood very close to Jonathan, and as she examined the items on the floor, she contorted her body in unnecessary ways and bumped into Jonathan on several occasions. All her movements seemed calculated to expose all areas of her body that were not covered by cloth.

The visitors took full advantage of the show

while they ruminate about the possible reasons for this extreme dress and behavior. Was she simply there to provide entertainment or was she trying to distract them, so they may not detect some deficiencies in the contents of the warehouse? Little did Veronica know that that was a minor issue. The major thing Jonathan and Dani were interested in was the C-4. The rest of the weaponry was only of secondary importance.

"I see nothing here out of the ordinary," Veronica announced. "So please, do your business and let me know when you are finished."

Dani and Jonathan proceeded with clipboard in hand, to do the necessary inventory and the elaborate wrapping and sealing of the pile of C-4. While they worked, the nearly-naked nymph navigated narrow niches, and nearly nudged numerous nearby, neatly-numbered, nasty munitions, as she pirouetted and gyrated through several ballet and gymnastic movements for the astounded visitors. The artistic movements were periodically interrupted as she seductively stroked Jonathan's arm, and gruffly poked Dani's. Jonathan stole glances at the sweet young thing and thought, *what a waste it will be to blow her up.*

None of the inspector's actions were challenged, and upon finishing, they informed Veronica and recited the contract requirements that the winning host must adhere to post-auction. She continued her gyrations while they awaited a response. Walking on her hands while circling the visitors was of particular interest. Shortly, she righted herself and said with a smile, "Your demands have been agreed to. It has been fun spending time with you today. The guards will show you out."

Before leaving, Jonathan stammered, "Thank

you for being here…for performing for us. It made our job much more enjoyable."

The young woman giggled, cocked her head, looked up through long painted eyelashes and said sweetly, "Why, thank you, Mr. Broxton." Then she gave Dani a nasty look and shook her fanny in Dani's direction.

When they got to their car, Dani and Jonathan looked at each other in dumbfounded amusement before Dani said, "What was that all about?"

Jonathan shrugged and replied, "Damned if I know, but it was fun. She knew my last name so I guess there must be more to her than meets the eye… so to speak."

When they arrived back at the hotel, Roger and Henry were already partaking refreshments. Dani and Jonathan joined right in while relating the strangeness of their encounter. They all laughed about the incident and prayed for the safety of the nearly naked-nymph, but wondered what they were missing. Somehow, it felt as if something would come back to haunt them on the big day tomorrow.

CHAPTER ELEVEN

Everyone spent a fitful night and was up at dawn preparing breakfast, incessantly drinking coffee, while making final preparations for the culmination of their efforts and planning for the last few months: the weapons auction.

Their first action was to send an email to all participants reminding them that this was the big day, and that all bids must be submitted by 1PM, again stating all of the requirements necessary for a winning bid. Of particular note was the requirement that the person- and the means for transferring funds to the winning bidder's bank account- must be present at the time of weapons pickup which would be approximately thirty minutes past the winner's notification. Acknowledgment of email receipt was requested, and eventually received from all bidders.

Unbeknownst to bidders, there was no intention of picking up the weaponry, just blowing the lot up along with the ultimate weapon's dealer. Therefore, there was no preparation in that regard.

Jonathan was in direct contact with the analytical, computer and security group just below them in the hotel. All parties concentrated on monitoring the secure Internet connections and the encrypted signals from the C-4 wrapped bundles, indicating they had not been tampered with. All signals were strong and consistent. Everything went well. However, there was tension that stifled any happy feelings or the desire to celebrate. That must wait until the big bang, because of the complexity of the situation, they knew that the project's status could change at any moment. They all sat with sweaty faces before computer monitors in order to detect any abnormal information so that appropriate action could be taken if necessary.

Amidst all the tension, Henry spoke up, "Damn! This is just too nerve racking, so I'm going to relieve it with, not a limerick but a regular poem. I have been working on this for a special occasion, and now seems appropriate. Here goes:

As the chase began, the ending was as certain as sunrise.
The victim strained her utmost, to elude, deceive, surprise.
Inevitably, the stalker closed and struck; teeth penetrating deeply.
Slowly the victim turned, eyes meeting pursuer's intently.
Not pleading for freedom from this encounter's ordained ending.
But demanding a quick end to the pain and humiliation pending.
No time to reflect on or validate a life not so long ago extruded.
A life randomly conceived, randomly lived, and now randomly concluded."

Before anyone could say anything, Dani piped up, "Yours is very elegant. Henry and I know I should just let it ride, but a challenge is a challenge, and so here is my meager offering:

> *Life is a wondrous thing to behold,*
> *A series of interlocking scenes that unfold.*
> *One wonders if his life is worthwhile,*
> *Or simply a mosaic painted in tile.*
> *All is concealed until your history is told."*

"Very nice, guys. That was a welcome interlude, and both poems give us something to think about other than our mission," Jonathan responded.

"Yeah," Roger added. "Yeah, that was sweet. You guys are really getting good at this poetry thing. I like it."

Jonathan, being in charge of the entire operation, was responsible for lifting the red receiver and dialing the number that would simultaneously detonate the C-4 bundles at all locations. Confirmation of successful detonation at each site was to be displayed on all monitors and that was the signal that everyone eagerly awaited. The four of them sat in silence, breathed deeply, and prepared themselves for the next step.

As the clock struck 1PM, Jonathan polled all the good guys to determine if they knew of anything that would prevent him from proceeding to detonation. Hearing none at 1:05PM, Jonathan raised the receiver and dialed the magic number.

After a thirty second delay, the sites began to confirm detonation. However, they had no visual confirmation of the explosions. For that, they had to wait for the 911 calls to newspapers, TV stations, police stations, and homeland security.

Only minutes after the first detonation the calls started coming in and the group began recording the tally. Once a particular site's detonation was reported by two different sources, it was recorded as successful. It took several minutes before visual confirmation became available for display on local TV. The group eagerly watched the extent of the damage in order to estimate the percentage of weapons that had been destroyed, a number that they would have to confirm personally in the days to come.

For a full hour, all members of the group were silent and circumspect. They looked with blank faces at their monitors and each other in recognition of the enormity of what they had done. Enthusiasm was dampened because parts of them wished to celebrate while other parts were sad for the loss of life and property. They felt they could be satisfied with their accomplishment, but at the same time they felt morally reprehensible. To destroy people and property wantonly was not a good thing in general.

They had to weigh the good; getting rid of evil people and weapons of destruction versus the actual killing and chaos. Were their actions morally on the plus side or on the negative side? Each of the group pondered the issues, and in time began shifting their self-respect in the positive direction.

One by one, the group members rose from their chairs and monitors, and met in the center of the room hugging each other and saying, "Job well done." Finally, a spirit of joy pervaded the room. It was only then that all four members of the good guys, as Jonathan liked to think of his merry band of friends, began to celebrate. They called down to the kitchen for some fine of unhealthy food to fill their yearning gullets and facilitate their celebration.

While they awaited their food, they opened two bottles of wine and filled their glasses. They sat down to leisurely review the continuing reports from TV and Homeland Security, and to quantify the devastation to assess the success of their mission.

About a half hour later, there was a knock on the door. Jonathan said on his way to the door, "The food must be here. Let's get ready to rumble." Little did he know how appropriate that statement was.

He gladly flung open the door but was subsequently knocked to the floor by the first of two carts of food. The two people pushing the carts leaped into the room and shot several rounds from their AK47's into the ceiling and concurrently shouted, "Everyone get down on the floor right now or the next rounds will find some flesh and bones!"

The good guys were frozen by the sudden change from elation and celebration to fear and confusion, causing them to slowly respond affirmatively to the attackers' demands. Two additional invaders rolled out from the lower shelf of the food carts, each brandishing their own weapons. "I said, move! NOW!" the leader shouted. It was a female voice Jonathan and Dani were familiar with. She ripped off the chef's hat and white coat which were stolen from the real food deliverers somewhere between the kitchen and Jonathan's floor. A very low tech method for infiltrating what Jonathan previously thought was a highly secure facility.

The leader turned out to be Veronica, but this time she was not dressed as the nearly naked nymph but as a lethally armed terrorist in a black jumpsuit. As if to keep in character, the jumpsuit was unzipped to the navel. She shot several more rounds into the ceiling and demanded everyone to the floor immediately and everyone complied.

Once all of the terrorists were strategically positioned and the good guys were on the floor,

Veronica began to trash the room with the butt of her gun and the others chimed in until the room looked as if it had been bombed. They then went throughout the floor trashing everything in sight with the butts of their guns as well as bullets. It was a sickening feeling for Jonathan to see everything he valued be destroyed so wantonly, and his anger and desire for revenge nearly caused him to burst into action. However, his experience told him that action at this point had only a small chance of success, and so, he waited for a better opportunity.

When the entire floor was trashed, the invaders congregated in the same room as the devastated, frightened but slowly regrouping good guys.

Veronica poked Dani with the butt of her rifle and said, "Get your ass in that chair, you dirty little boy."

Dani slowly rose from the floor and tried to

find a reasonably comfortable position in a highly tattered chair as she brushed debris from her body and the chair. Before she was completely settled Veronica delivered a hard blow to Dani's face with an open hand. She stood over Dani, menacingly waiting for a possible reply as she said, "I told you that I would see you again. I knew you were up to no good. Now, you have destroyed my warehouse and everything in it, and I've come to do the same to you, but with a slight difference. You won't be walking away from here alive."

Dani held up her hand in a peace offering and pleaded with Veronica, "We didn't have anything to do with any destruction. Please let's talk about it."

Veronica delivered another slap and said, "You're a liar! I know what you did."

Dani could see by her actions that this whole thing was very personal to Veronica, and her feelings seemed to be focused on her. She guessed that Veronica must have some sort of attraction to her and that's why she struck her with her open hand rather than take the very impersonal approach; simply shooting her. So, she decided to play to that as she said, "No! Please Veronica, you are a very beautiful, young woman. Why can't we just kiss and make up?"

Veronica responded with, "Just like you to say something like that just to get out of trouble." But Dani noticed that her mood mellowed slightly and the anger lines in her face softened, so Dani continued, "We could sit together and talk and get to know each other better. I think I could convince you that we had nothing to do with the destruction of your warehouse. I like you too much for that."

Veronica's grip on her gun relaxed slightly and her lips showed a barely discernible smile, but she remained silent.

Dani reached out and gently grasped Veronica's hand as she said, "You don't really want to hurt me, and I feel more like caressing you than hurting you. Can't we just talk this out, friend to friend?"

Veronica didn't pull her hand away and the two of them stayed with hands clasped as she struggled desperately to weigh whether she believed Dani. The effort could be seen in her contorted face and erratic body movements. After several minutes, she reached a decision, and threw Dani's hand aside, raised the butt of her gun in an attempt to deliver a crushing blow to Dani's head as she shouted, "You liar! I'm going to kill you!"

"Before you can do that, I'm going to rearrange your face!" Dani screamed back as she rotated her body and swiftly raised her leg immediately behind Veronica's arm to redirect the blow and accelerate its force, so that Veronica lost control of the rifle. It sailed across the room and Veronica fell to one knee.

Dani quickly rose and attempted to deliver a kick to Veronica's head, but she nimbly brushed it aside and they engaged in battle with a succession of karate hits and kicks. Dani seemed to be overly matched as they engaged each other.

Veronica's flying rifle narrowly missed the villain who was standing near Henry. When he ducked to evade the sailing rifle, Henry quickly retrieved his lethal lead-filled cane and smashed the assailant's knee cap, dropping him to his knees. This provided Henry an opportunity to deliver a more lethal blow to the assailant's head. When you take the legs out from under an assailant, the battle is virtually over. Then, a powerful blow to the head can end the struggle quite dramatically. Henry secured the bad guy's weapon and slid himself to a sitting position against the wall. There, he sat ready to strike or shoot any bad guy that came into his range, and yet, stay reasonably safe from the more agile combatants. From this vantage point, he studied the battle between Dani and Veronica with fascination. He felt that Veronica was stronger and had the advantage in what appeared to be a battle to the death.

As the punches and kicks continued, sweat mixed with blood and was colored again by passion as the lady warriors exchanged blow after blow. Henry could see Veronica's superiority begin slipping away as Dani delivered one decisive blow after another. In time, Veronica's slaps turned into seeming caresses, her karate holds became hugs, and her response to Dani's leg kicks became opportunities to grab Dani randomly. It became an even battle, and each combatant became wounded but still, the ambiguous contest continued. In the midst of battle, the image of the nearly naked nymph returned as her black jump suit became tattered to expose her exquisite anatomy and she seemed to enjoy Dani's blows to her body rather than to suffer from them.

The flying rifle and Henry's devastating blows were like igniting a pile of C-4 for Roger and Jonathan, each springing so swiftly to attack mode that the bad guys were unable to respond with their weapons in a meaningful way, harmlessly shooting the ceiling or floor while receiving blow after blow from Jonathan and Roger.

Shortly, the room was filled with flying bodies and random debris. It would be futile to attempt to describe individual battles because of their number and the fact that assailants constantly changed; one attacked whomever was in his vicinity. Henry's blows and stabs with his cane shortened several battles. The carnage continued as long as the good guys could discern the bad guys and not inadvertently strike another good guy.

Finally, Dani's last karate kick laid Veronica vanquished face down on the floor, with Dani sitting astride her with one of Veronica's hands twisted painfully behind her back. Dani felt proud of her conquest of an opponent which she felt initially to be a superior physical specimen, and she gritted her teeth as she twisted Veronica's arm with all the strength she had left. She skipped the primordial scream, and her habit of pirouetting and blowing kisses to her adoring fans. She was too determined to hang on to the cinch rope and not be knocked off this wild bronco. She was just too damn exhausted to go another round and was thankful that the battle was seemingly at an end.

On the other hand, Veronica seemed to accept

the fact that she was defeated by *'the dirty little boy.'* Covered equally with blood, sweat, cuts, and bruises, she struggled against the pain of her twisted arm, but she managed a satisfied smile. Yes, she had lost this battle and all of her munitions, the warehouse and her personal freedom was uncertain, but she laid there nearly naked on the floor with Dani riding her like a pony while holding her hand. Under the circumstances, at least temporarily this was a conclusion that she could live with. If she was to join Dani and Henry's poetry challenge she might have written the following:

> *"Here I lie face down in my own blood and sweat,*
> *An unlikely circumstance I would have bet.*
> *Being defeated by a beautiful but physically*
> *inferior being,*
> *Has enhanced my introspective seeing.*
> *I now feel her intimate touch as salve to my*
> *anguish set."*

The pandemonium swung steadily in favor of the good guys, 'till in the end, all of them were still standing, if battered and bruised, and all the terrorists lay supine on the debris strewn floor.

The battle was won by the time security forces arrived. They placed the bad guys in handcuffs, and hauled them off to jail, while the good guys righted whatever chair they could find and between visits to the shattered remains of the food cart they sat. They munched and drank wine while congratulating each other on a job well done.

Roger was singled out and Jonathan thanked him for his brief but game-changing assistance and received Roger's promise that if needed he would only be too happy to help the group in the future.

When evening came and the desire for sleep overtook them, they found other accommodations in the hotel for a well-deserved shower and rest. Roger and Dani went off together to share a room. It appeared to everyone that this had transitioned to a potentially long- lasting relationship. Of course, Henry could see this and was upset, even angry as he said his *"hum bugs"* and *"shits"* silently to himself. He had become very fond of this young woman, and here, this young whipper-snapper came in and took her away. He understood the situation intellectually, but he cried emotionally. And then, there was Jonathan who was quite proud of what his newly-formed family had accomplished this last few months. The way they handled the just-completed battle had been most satisfying. But he was exhausted, cut, bruised, and his entire body was in pain from the beating he absorbed during the battle even though he had come out a winner. He drew himself a hot bath, disrobed, and jumped in the tub with a bottle of Port. He then settled in to consider the great questions of mankind: *Who am I? Where did I come from? Why am I here? And Where am I going?*

The first question was always the most difficult for Jonathan and had perplexed him for most of his adult years. The question of who he was became more acute as he examined the cuts and bruises from the battle, and memories flooded his mind from an earlier fierce encounter that had changed his life. He saw the fifteen-year-old Jennifer cut through the park one day on her way home from school. She was accosted there by four teenage boys and dragged her behind some bushes. There they ripped off most of her clothes and repeatedly raped her. She fought them with everything she had, but finally fell unconscious and the assault continued until the boys grew tired of, or perhaps disgusted with what they were doing.

When Jennifer awoke, it was dark and she found herself in total disarray, bruised, bleeding and in agonizing pain. She couldn't accept the condition she was in and just wanted to die. She held her breath until her bodily needs overcame her will, and her lungs drew in new air. She closed her eyes and prayed that when she awoke all that had happened to her had been a nightmare. But each time she opened her eyes, she was confronted by reality and despair overtook her. She felt less than human, more like a piece of furniture that people could use and then throw away.

As a last resort, she gathered together what was left of her clothes, put them on and made her way home where Henry met her. She wasn't the Jennifer he knew. Those parasites somehow stole her identity and now, she didn't know who she was. She appeared to be more like a wounded animal who displayed a profound neediness, yet a creature feeling not worth being helped. Without saying a word, Henry picked her up in his arms and made his way to the bathroom. He set her on the toilet and supported her as he drew a warm bath. He then removed all of her clothes and placed her in the warm water where he soaped her up, and tenderly washed away the accumulated dirt and blood. He told her that he understood what had happened, and that she didn't have to give details until she was ready. However, days and weeks tumbled by, but she never became ready to describe what had happened. She no longer wanted to be a girl because bad things happen to girls. She began dressing like a boy, cut her hair like a boy, and eventually asked to be called Jonathan.

All the while, Henry counseled her against the new identity but didn't compel her not to do it. He tried to provide home schooling and a receptive ear for her. In time, they became father and son. They proceeded through life as such. Over time, together, they systematically tracked down the four boys and destroyed them.

The memories were still fresh on Jonathan's mind when he rose from the bath and stood before the mirror, and began to reflect upon the image that stared back at him. However, this time the cuts, bruises and pain he received during the just concluded battle were not in vain. He emerged victorious against a stronger man. That seemed to enable him to find and occupy Jennifer's long lost identity. Before him stood a beautifully packaged, adult, Jennifer. After a long and thoughtful reflection, he made his way to the chest of drawers in the bedroom where he had long ago stashed makeup and a wig of long flowing blond curls for just such an occasion. He put the wig on as he made his way back to the mirror and then continued to complete the picture of who he really was by applying lipstick, mascara and the associated facial treatments. Then, he stood back to examine the results. Except for all the bruises and cuts received during the battle, he liked what he saw and began to question why Jonathan still needed to exist.

Following another long examination of the image in the mirror, he said to himself, "This is who I am. This is who I will be for the rest of my life. I don't have to pretend that I'm a man any longer. Damn it! This is what nature intended in the first place, and now I see no reason to continue to run away from it. Jonathan's Secret is dead. Starting tomorrow, Jennifer Broxton will walk out of here to continue the life that Jonathan deprived her of for so long, and Henry can have his precious little girl back again."

****

In the morning Jennifer slipped on a tight fitting dress with a plunging neckline, her flowing blond wig, and the appropriate face makeup. She examined herself in the mirror for a very long time. She then said to herself, "It's time to start my new life.

I will never again wear Jonathan's mask." She then bound into the front room where Henry, Danni and Roger were attempting to straighten up after the battle of last night, saying, "Jennifer is back. I came to help the cleanup!"

Henry was the first to respond saying, "Jennifer! Jennifer is that you?

Jennifer replied, "Yes. It's me, daddy, and I'm not going away ever again!"

They ran for each other and hugged each other as if their life depended on it, and the tears flowed uncontrollably. All the while Roger and Danni could only stare with their mouths wide open and feel the love that was being displayed before them not knowing who this young lady was.

In time the love birds broke up and Henry yelled, "Let's go down and have breakfast. Let's talk about what had just happened here. What do you say?"

All he heard were a wild series of yes's, and they came together in a giant hug!

THE END

www.ingramcontent.com/pod-product-compliance
Lightning Source LLC
Chambersburg PA
CBHW061259210726
48293CB00003B/1028